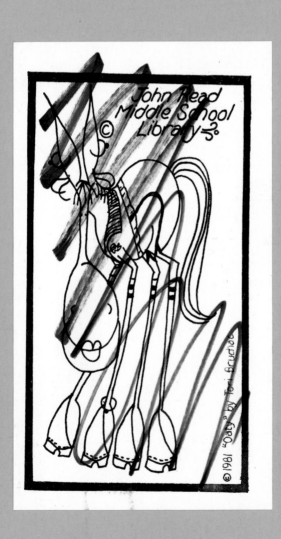

Playing
Murder

also by Sandra Scoppetone

Trying Hard to Hear You
The Late Great Me
Happy Endings Are All Alike
Long Time Between Kisses
Some Unknown Person
Such Nice People
Innocent Bystanders

AND WITH LOUISE FITZHUGH
Suzuki Beane
Bang Bang You're Dead

Playing
Murder

A NOVEL BY

Sandra Scoppettone

1 8 1 7

———— HARPER & ROW, PUBLISHERS ————

Cambridge, Philadelphia, San Francisco, London, Mexico City, São Paolo, Singapore, Sydney

———— NEW YORK ————

Grateful acknowledgement is made to Sarah Kartalia for the use of her poem on page 108

Playing Murder
Copyright © 1985 by Sandra Scoppettone
All rights reserved. No part of this book may be used or reproduced in any manner whatsoever without written permission except in the case of brief quotations embodied in critical articles and reviews. Printed in the United States of America. For information address Harper & Row, Publishers, Inc., 10 East 53rd Street, New York, N.Y. 10022. Published simultaneously in Canada by Fitzhenry & Whiteside Limited, Toronto.
Designed by Joyce Hopkins
1   2   3   4   5   6   7   8   9   10
First Edition

Library of Congress Cataloging in Publication Data
Scoppettone, Sandra.
  Playing Murder.

  Summary: When one of the players in a murder game is killed, seventeen-year-old Anna and her twin brother realize that their circle of friends may conceal a real murderer.
  [1. Twins—Fiction.   2. Mystery and detective stories]   I. Title.
PZ7.S4136Pl   1985   [Fic]   83-47707
ISBN 0-06-025283-9
ISBN 0-06-025284-7 (lib. bdg.)

This one is for Amy and Annie Crawford

And Sarah Wood

1

They ran. You could hear the thumping of their feet on the ground, the swishing of tall grass as they scurried away. Three minutes was all they had. A matter of life and death.

A cool north wind rustled the tops of trees, and the quarter moon, apricot yellow, floated in the sky, a flurry of clouds crossing its path. The light it cast was dim, illuminating very little.

The seconds ticked away into a minute. Gone. Two left. A cracking sound. A grunt. A thud. Someone had fallen over a branch, snapped it in two. The running continued. Heavy breathing, panting.

The wind kicked up. Leaves whirled into faces. The air chilled. Another minute gone. One left.

In the sky a streak of lightning, some distance away, scored the black night like a luminous ribbon, then vanished. But it had been enough light to see some of them, if only for an instant. Enough light to seek and find and destroy.

The third minute ticked its last second. The shrill whistle resonated in their ears and they knew the end had come. Everyone stopped still. Only the wind was a constant now and the confident treading of one pair of feet. The crackle of twigs, the reshuffling of underbrush deafening in the hush of the night.

Another slice of lightning, closer now. And then, seconds later, the dull sound of thunder. Rain hadn't been predicted. Would it make a difference? A little rain? Why would rain stop the inevitable? Again the flashing, lighting up the woods, making every tree, every branch look like long thin arms with gnarled fingers ready to reach out and twist, claw, strangle.

A second whistle. Silence. Then it came, the expected. But even so it shocked. A scream in the night, long and piercing, causing shortness of breath, skittering hearts and sweaty palms. The sound went on, curling sharply upward, then abruptly it stopped. For a second there was nothing, as if time itself had ceased. But with the next splash of light, followed almost at once by a crash of thunder, reality refocused. It was at that moment they faced the truth.

One of them had been murdered.

2

I keep looking back, trying to figure it out. Were there clues? If I'd been on my toes would I have noticed anything suspicious or unusual during the day or early evening? We'd been playing the game for almost a month. Was there anything different about last night? Of course there was the weather. We should have known it was going to rain, to thunder and to lightning. But really what difference did that make in the end? The weather hadn't made it happen. So why? And who? It just didn't make sense.

We should never have come to Blue Haven Island in the first place. It was all Bill's fault, all because of him. Mom and Dad wouldn't have made the move, even though they said they'd been thinking about it for a long time. They would never have made me miss my senior year. Well, I know they were glad to get me away from Tony, but after the summer that would have happened anyway. No, it was Bill's fault. He didn't care about anything or anyone but himself. But it hadn't always been that way. Bill used to be a great guy; everyone loved him, especially me.

The old cliché, two peas in a pod, described us perfectly. It wasn't that we looked alike, although our coloring was the same; it was more that we thought alike, viewed the world in similar ways. See, Bill and I are twins. Fraternal twins, of course. Only same-sex twins can be identical.

From the beginning Bill and I were more than friends, more than brother and sister. It was almost as if we were one person. Mom said when we were babies we always got hungry at exactly the same time, just as we always cried at the same moment even if we were in different parts of the house. Then when we got older and started to talk, we finished each other's sentences because we thought alike almost all the time and each of us knew what the other was feeling.

And then he changed. We grew apart. He wouldn't talk to me anymore. In fact, he sometimes acted like I was his enemy instead of his best friend, and that took its toll on me. His withdrawal and strangeness started in our sophomore year and gradually escalated until the horrible incident in the early part of our junior year.

It's funny how one thing can lead to so many others. Like a chain reaction. If Bill had been taller he probably wouldn't have had any girl trouble, and he might not have needed to cry out for attention, like the psychologist told Mom and Dad. Then he wouldn't have stolen all the money for the football uniforms and we wouldn't have had to move, and then . . . But the murder would have happened anyway, because neither Bill nor I did it. Still, we wouldn't have known about it because we'd be safe in our old house in our old town. But we're not. All because my twin brother is only five feet four inches tall and isn't going to grow anymore.

Aside from Bill's height the crummy chain of events began more than seven months ago. I remember that night in January as if it were engraved on my memory. We were sitting in the family room—Mom, Dad, Bill, Kate and me.

"Are you listening, Anna?" my father asked.

"Yes, Dad." I was listening, all right, but I wasn't believing it. Who could?

My mother said, "You look like you're dreaming, honey."

"I'm listening, okay?" She was about to get on my case, so I stared at my father like a good little girl, listening and paying close attention as he outlined the ruination of everything I'd dreamed and hoped for.

"So do any of you have any questions?" Dad asked.

My little sister, Kate, said, "When do we go?"

"As soon as school's out."

"You mean," Kate asked, her green eyes getting watery, "I won't be going to camp?"

"Not this year, sweetie," Mom said.

Kate's lower lip trembled but she held back bravely. She was a pretty grown-up kid for an eleven-year-old.

I looked over at Bill. He was slumping in the big overstuffed chair we all fought to sit in when we watched the tube. His red hair (both he and I had inherited that from Mom, but only Kate had gotten her green eyes) was a little grungy looking, like he'd sweated a lot and hadn't washed it. Maybe his guilty conscience had made him sweat. I started fuming.

"What's going on with you, Anna?" Dad asked. "You look like you're going to explode."

"I just might," I said.

"So let's hear it."

"Will it change anything?"

"It might," he said.

"Like leaving here?"

"Well, no."

"That's what I thought." I put my head on my knees, which were pulled up tight against my chest.

"We don't express what's on our minds just to get our own way," Dad said. Sometimes he sounded so teacherish. I guess it was in his marrow.

I said, "I never get my own way. I'm a middle child and that's the worst."

Mom said, "A middle child? How do you figure that?"

"I was born two minutes after Bill, wasn't I?"

"Now I've heard everything," Mom said, laughing.

"Come on, Glamor," Dad said, "spill the beans."

"Oh, Dad," I said, embarrassed by his use of my old nickname. When I was eight I got into my mother's makeup and painted my face with lipstick, blush and eye shadow. I thought I looked beautiful, but I guess I looked like some kind of crazy clown. Anyway, Dad started calling me Glamorpuss after that and then it got short-

6

ened to Glamor. But I suppose that's better than if he called me Puss.

"Look," he went on, "I know you must be disappointed about not having your senior year at Columbia, but sometimes we have to make sacrifices for others."

I looked over at Bill. He was still scrunched way down in his chair, his pointy chin on his chest. "You mean I have to give up everything I've dreamed of because my brother's a thief!"

"Anna!" Mom said.

"Well, it's true." And it was. I'd tried not to be angry with Bill for what he'd done, but the facts were the facts. He'd stolen the money, which caused everyone embarrassment, and now that act was messing up all my plans.

We had a whole lot of back and forth then, with both of them trying to pretend that it didn't have anything to do with Bill, that they'd been wanting to do this for a long time, but we kids knew better. Finally, after a look passed between my parents, the kind only grownups have with each other, Dad told the truth.

"Okay, Anna, you win. Yes, we *have* decided to make this change at this time because of Bill. And for you. If we stay here in Maplewood, senior year will be hell for both of you. As it is you've got to get through five and a half months with everyone in school knowing what he did."

"It just isn't fair," I said.

Bill made a grunting noise and I looked over at him. He was still looking down at his sneakers.

"What's that supposed to mean, Bill?" Dad asked.

He didn't answer.

I knew anyway. And for a second—just a second—I felt sorry for him. If anybody knew about things not being fair, I guess he did. For example, having a twin sister who was three inches taller than you.

Mom said, "Things have always been pretty good for you, Anna, pretty fair. Maybe now you're going to have to learn to roll with the punches."

"Even when I don't start the punching?" I asked.

"Even then," she said, running a hand through her curly, red hair.

Suddenly Bill jumped out of his chair like one of those old Jack-in-the-boxes. "Listen, I'm not going to take the rap for this move," he yelled. "I'm perfectly willing to stay here and take the consequences. It's you two"—he pointed to Mom and Dad—"who can't take the heat, and you just want to dump it all on me." He stood there shaking, his hands clenched in fists at his sides.

I wondered if what he said was true. After all, Dad was a teacher at Columbia, and both my parents were very social with their country club and all their friends. Maybe they *were* ashamed and couldn't face anyone.

"I bet he's right," I said, jumping on Bill's bandwagon, and for a moment it made me feel like it was old times when we used to think and do everything alike.

"I won't deny that I'd rather not go on teaching where my son is known as a thief."

"Jack!" Mom said.

"Oh, Sally, for God's sake stop reacting to the word *thief*. It's what he is. It's what he did. And you don't want to face people because of it any more than I do."

So it *was* the truth. And just a few minutes before, he was giving us this big line of bull about how the move was for us. Bill and I exchanged a look of our own, then he went back and flopped in his chair, disgusted.

"Well, you haven't been very honest about all this," I said. I don't like people to get away with things.

Dad's face was looking pretty flushed and his eyes had that flash of light they got when he was mad.

"I don't need you to tell me that, Anna. We didn't have to call this family meeting. And we didn't have to tell you now. We could have waited, but we wanted you to have a chance to adjust to the idea, make any plans you need to make. Naturally we didn't expect rave reviews for this venture, but you're not even giving it a chance. Maine's a beautiful place, and we used to have some of our best times there, remember?"

"No," Kate said, "I don't."

"Well, maybe you wouldn't," Dad said.

We hadn't been back to Maine since Dad's parents died and Mom's mother (NuNu to us) moved to Florida. That was more than six years ago.

"You remember, don't you, Anna?"

I did and told him so.

"Don't you remember how much fun it was?"

"Dad, I was Kate's age . . . younger even."

"You don't have to say it like it's something dirty to be," Kate said.

"I didn't mean it that way," I said apologetically. "I just meant that at eleven everything is fun."

"Gee," Kate said, "I can hardly wait to be a teenager so everything will be boring."

9

"I'm not saying this right. What I mean is that I won't know anyone and there just won't be anything to do."

"Oh, yes there will," Mom said. She was laughing again.

"What's so funny?" I asked.

"Nothing. I'm sorry."

"Well, what did you mean, 'Oh, yes there will'?"

"She meant that there'll be plenty to do on Blue Haven Island because we're going there for a specific reason," Dad said.

All three of us kids looked at each other, then back at Mom and Dad waiting for an explanation.

"You'd better tell them, Jack. Boy, I can't wait for this reaction."

I guess I could liken the feeling I had then to one of complete and total dread, like the one I have as I lower my butt into the dentist's chair, only at that moment I would have preferred three hours' worth of torture by Dr. Jacob to hearing whatever it was that my father was about to tell us. But I didn't have a choice.

"I know," Kate said brightly, "we're going to become a rock group."

Kate was always trying for laughs.

"Har de har har," Bill and I said at the same time, and then we really laughed. For a moment I'd forgotten how mad at him I was. Then I remembered and looked away.

"What are we going to do, Dad? The suspense is killing me," I said.

"We're going to work," he said.

"WORK?" This came from all three of us.

"Your mother and I have bought a restaurant—an

10

outdoor restaurant where you have clambakes. We're all going to work there. And we're going to have fun; we're going to have a wonderful time."

Some wonderful time! Well, I'll have to admit a lot of it *was* fun. Even though the work was hard—Blue Haven Island, our house, the beach, our new friends, playing the game—all of it was fun until last night. Now fun seemed as remote as the moon. Because nothing can be fun when you know that one of your friends is a killer!

3

We didn't get home until after midnight. Everybody was a wreck. Mom and Dad had been called by the police, and they had come to get me and Bill, bringing Kate with them. When we got back to the house we had some milk and some of Dad's blueberry pie. Dad's a great baker. Tonight everybody just picked at it, though. We couldn't eat after what had happened. So we just sat around the table and Mom and Dad told us how much they loved us. I guess they were grateful it wasn't either of us who got killed. We all felt really close, closer than we had in a long time. When we said good night, we kissed and hugged a lot, something we hadn't done since before Bill stole the money. Why is it that other people's tragedies bring you closer together? I realized then how much I'd missed the loving family we'd once been. I guess when I don't have something, I tell myself I don't miss it and I don't . . . until I have it back again.

I flopped on my bed in my clothes. I knew it would be better to change into my pj's, but I just didn't have the energy. Every part of my body ached with tiredness. And my mind felt as if I'd been slammed with a two-by-four. There was a sense of unreality to everything— even my room in the dark seemed strange. The rain had stopped hours before, but the night was still dim, no moon or stars to illuminate anything. Still, I could see my chair, my desk, the trunk in the corner of the room. But even so, that weird sense of everything being unreal continued. I turned over and closed my eyes. I thought back to five weeks before.

As much as I tried not to feel frightened about our move, I still did. There's nothing worse than not knowing what lies ahead. Like now. I don't have any idea of what will happen next; nobody does. I've never been connected to a murder before, but I know a little bit about it because my mother is a mystery writer and I read all her books. You can learn a lot that way. Even so, reading is one thing and life is another and having that extra knowledge didn't stop me from feeling afraid. For one thing there is the very real possibility that the killer will do it again, so everything and everyone becomes threatening. But that's a very different kind of fear from the one I had before the move.

Then I was scared of a lot of dumb things like: Would I make friends, what would the island be like, the restaurant, would Bill do something awful again, would I be lonely? Had I known what lay ahead, those fears would have seemed like nothing. But there was no way

I could have imagined what was going to happen, and if somehow I'd had a presentiment, no one would have believed me. I wouldn't have believed it myself. But I didn't know, so I just went on being scared about a lot of jerky things. Some of those fears were allayed our first day on Blue Haven Island.

Now that's another thing. Blue Haven Island. It doesn't seem like an island at all because it's so big. It has seventeen mountains and five large lakes and a national park that is sixteen miles wide and thirteen miles long. The biggest and swankiest town on the island is Cranberry Harbor. It has lots of shops and restaurants and a yacht club, and very rich people go there. But you'd never know you were on an island.

The day we arrived I was driving with Mom and Kate. Bill and Dad were in a rented truck behind us with some of our stuff. Most of it had gone into storage, because this was going to be a one-year experiment. Now who knows? Anyway, that day Mom said:

"Well, kids, we're on the island."

I said, "If I remember correctly from geography, an island is a piece of land surrounded by a body of water."

"Right," said Mom.

"So where's the body?" asked Kate.

"Didn't you see the water when we passed over the bridge back there?"

"What bridge?" I asked.

"I have to admit," Mom said, "it wasn't your ordinary from-the-mainland-to-the-island-type bridge, but it *was* a bridge."

Both Kate and I turned around, but we'd gone too

far to see anything but the immediate road behind us.

I was still trying to get the feel of being on an island when I heard Mom say:

"Our road."

I glanced at the sign: Water Street. Very imaginative, I thought. The road itself was real bumpy, and I could hear the truck behind us thumping and clacking as it followed us. We seemed to be going down a kind of incline, and I noticed one house on the right and then no more. The road twisted to the left, and when we came around the next bend it straightened out and there ahead of us was the water.

It was a gorgeous June day, the sun all crisp-looking, and the sky, an azure blue, was cloudless. And as much as I was feeling bereft and lonely and scared, I couldn't help my spirits rising as I took in that cool blue-green water that lapped against the rocks in little foamy spumes.

Mom slowed way down and took a left.

"There it is," she said.

The house. Our house. I couldn't believe how neat-looking it was, and how big. Mom and Dad had come up here in March and picked it out. We'd been told that the house was called the Red Door, and now I could see why. Simple. It had a large red door! In fact, the whole house was red and white like a big candy cane or a barbershop pole. And it actually had a white picket fence around it.

Mom stopped the car near the fence, and we jumped out just as Dad and Bill pulled up next to us. We all stood around staring at the house as if we were afraid to go in.

15

"Well, let's start unloading," Dad said.

Mom said, "Wait a minute, Jack. Maybe the kids would like to go inside first."

The Red Door was unlocked, and we all trooped in behind Mom. When I saw the inside of our house, I felt better about everything right away. Sometimes, I guess, a house can do that, make you feel welcome, like you belong. This one sure did.

The living room was huge, with a big stone fireplace and an upright piano in a corner. The furnishings were all white wicker with gaily flowered cushions and matching curtains.

Beyond the living room was this big old kitchen with a stove that looked like it had been around since day one, and a crazy-looking refrigerator that had this round thing on top that could have been either a heater or an air conditioner or maybe neither.

"It's not something Julia Child would envy, but it's ours," Mom said about the kitchen.

"What's that thing on top of the fridge?" Kate asked.

Dad said, "That's the motor."

"For a minute there," Bill said, "I thought maybe it was a reject from Cape Canaveral."

We all laughed, and some of the tension we'd been feeling broke. The other two rooms downstairs were a big dining room and a guest bedroom. Then we went upstairs.

The rooms weren't huge or anything but they were a nice size and had iron bed frames and old chests. And best of all, they each had a water view. Naturally, Mom and Dad got the biggest and Kate the smallest. My room was the same size as Bill's and right next door. The bathroom was large with a tub that had funny claw feet. In the hall was a door we hadn't opened.

"What's this?" I asked.

"It goes to the attic," Dad said.

"What's up there?"

"It's unfinished," said Mom. "There's a cot and a small chest, but I'm sure it gets very hot midsummer. We won't be using it."

That day seems ages ago, but only five weeks have passed. Five weeks of a new life. Will it all be over now? I thought of Kirk. Oh, Kirk.

The swishing sound of wind through the trees at the back of the house and the continuous crash of the surf below my window were beginning to make me sleepy. And then I heard the sound of the bell at the entrance to the harbor. Something about that sound brought me to a state of wakefulness again. I looked out the window and saw Cole's Light flashing across the sky every eight seconds. It made me feel safe, maybe because it never changed.

But now everything had changed. Only six hours had passed since the murder, but I knew nothing would ever be the same again.

How could Kirk be dead? I would never see him again. That seemed impossible. To never hear him laugh again, to never see his face, look into his kind eyes. I just couldn't comprehend it, couldn't absorb the reality of that. Tears were working their way up behind my eyes, and then I heard it.

A slow creaking sound.

I felt short-circuited, as if my blood had stopped running through my veins. I knew it wasn't the natural sounds of the old house—I had gotten used to them already. This was something else, something alien. I was afraid to turn over, to open my eyes, but keeping them shut was scary too.

And then it came again, the creaking.

This time, as though the sound had somehow entered me, I flipped over onto my back and half sat up, staring into the gray light.

The room was the same, nothing had changed.

Cre-ee-aa-kk!

I swiveled my head toward the closet and saw the door moving open.

Slowly, very slowly.

Was it the wind? But there *was* no wind. Someone was in there. Someone was hiding in my closet. Someone had gotten in there and was waiting for me. Waiting to kill me? I opened my mouth to scream.

And then came the voice.

"Anna?"

I drew in my breath. Was I going crazy? Had the night's events pushed me over some edge?

"Anna?"

I knew the voice. But it couldn't be.

The door opened even wider, swinging on its rusty hinges, and from the recess of the closet he stepped into my line of vision.

"Tony!" I said.

4

Tony and I had been going steady for two years. He was a year older than I and had graduated in June. In September he was going into the Air Force, and the goal we'd set was to be married in five years. I would be through with college then. Of course no one knew this except my best friend, Kristen, and his best friend, Pat. My parents would've had a fit if they'd known. Tony and I had planned to spend the summer together before he left, but moving up here had shot that down. Even though I'd known about the move since January, I hadn't told Tony until the beginning of June, the night of the senior prom.

I wore a great dress that was cream colored with little gray and purple flowers and a gray silk sash. Tony wore a burgundy tuxedo and a ruffled pink shirt. He gave me a beautiful corsage of pink roses and I gave him a boutonniere of one white rose. The theme of the dance was *Gone With the Wind,* and then there was this gazebo in the center of the gym made out of cardboard in the art classes. Streamers of crepe paper were strung from the top of it to the sides and corners of the room. It looked really excellent and the band was super. We'd been lucky enough to get The Snakepits, despite protests from some parents who thought they were disgusting. Sometimes adults can be such drags. What was the difference if the band members had snakes wound around their necks as long as the music was good?

Anyway, the prom was a great success and Tony and I had a terrific time. After the dance we went to a party at Pat's, Tony's best friend. Pat's mother had put out a buffet for us and we ate like pigs. The only sour note at the party was when Peter Hallahan made some remark to me about Bill's stealing the uniform money. He said it loud and in front of other people. It was a big downer. Tony told him to cool it and he did.

In the sixth grade, when height wasn't an issue, Bill had beat out Peter for captain of their Little League team, and Peter, who was one of those people who just had to be best at everything, had never forgotten it. He had made Bill's life miserable ever since the discovery of the theft, but it was the first time that I'd been embarrassed in public. Everyone knew about Bill but nobody had ever said anything uncool to me about it before.

After that we stayed at the party for another half hour and then decided to drive up to Short Hills and park in this place we'd found months before. We made out there a lot, nothing too heavy. Tony wanted to go all the way, but I didn't and he respected my wishes. If Mom and Dad had known that, they might have thought better of him, but it was hardly something I could have told them.

While we drove up the mountain, the news came on the radio and there was a report about this girl who'd hanged herself after having a fight with her boyfriend. It made me feel sick. I couldn't imagine doing something like that.

Tony said, "She must have really loved the guy."

"You think so?"

"Sure. Why else would she do that?"

"I don't know."

"I'd die for you," he said. "Wouldn't you die for me?"

"That wasn't dying *for* someone. It was *over* someone. There's a difference."

"Yeah, I guess."

The news report on top of Peter Hallahan's remark had put me in a rotten mood, and I dreaded telling Tony about the move to Maine but I knew I had to do it.

We pulled into our spot and Tony turned to me. I would have to tell him before we made out or I knew I never would.

"I have something to tell you," I said.

"You're pregnant!" He laughed, his straight, white teeth glistening in the moonlight.

"Very funny," I said, and slapped him on the arm.

"You've won a beauty queen contest and you're gonna go to Hollywood and become a star!"

"Oh, Tony, stop. Be serious."

"I *am* serious. You *could* be a movie star and you're *my* beauty queen."

He leaned toward me and took me in his arms. When his lips touched mine I felt myself melting into him, as always, and I almost forgot my resolve.

"No," I said, pushing him away.

His brown eyes narrowed. "Hey, I don't like that."

And I didn't like it when he acted tough. Tony was gorgeous, to put it mildly. He was very tall, almost six three, and had black, curly hair. He was the one who looked like a movie star, with his straight nose and full mouth and the one huge dimple in his right cheek. But when he got angry his looks changed and he got a dark cast around his eyes, as if he'd seen something hideous, something no one else could see. He looked that way a lot and some of his friends had taken to calling him Doctor Doom.

"Don't be Doctor Doom," I said.

"Listen, Anna, don't go telling me how to be, okay?"

I sighed. We weren't getting off to a good start.

"So what's the big deal? What've you got to tell me?"

I was scared of his reaction, but I'd waited too long as it was. "I don't know how to tell you this, Tony."

His face got even darker. "You gonna break up with me or somethin'?" he asked.

"Oh, no," I cried, and kissed his neck.

He relaxed a little and shrugged. "So what could be so bad then? Go on, tell me straight, whatever it is."

So I did. His face grew sad and I thought he might

22

cry even though I'd never seen him do that. Then he said:

"But our summer, our plans."

"I know." I reached out and put my hand on top of his.

"Is it 'cause of us?"

Tony knew how my parents felt about him, particularly my dad. "No, it's because of Bill."

"That wimp," he said, and banged the steering wheel so hard with the heel of his palm, it made me jump.

"Don't," I said.

"Why not? I'd like to kill that little creep."

"Tony, don't say that." I felt a pang of guilt ripple through me as I remembered having similar feelings the night I'd first heard about the move.

"Well, I would. Just because that sucker has problems, you gotta move and ruin our whole summer. I might as well go into the Force when I graduate." He slumped down in the seat and pulled a pack of cigarettes from his inside pocket.

"I thought you were quitting," I said.

"What the hell's the difference now?"

"I don't see what my move has to do with your smoking or not." People were always smoking for the dumbest reasons.

"Just shut up, I'm thinkin'."

That really made me mad. "No, I won't shut up. Why should I? Sometimes you're a real pig, Tony."

"And sometimes you're a royal pain in the butt."

"Take me home," I said.

"Gladly."

So that was how the big prom night ended. Well, that wasn't quite the end. There was one more lovely thing. After Tony pulled up short in front of our house, practically knocking me through the windshield, I slammed out of the car. Then he called to me as I walked up the path:

"Don't go hanging yourself now!"

It gave me the creeps.

But he phoned by noon the next day and we were all made up by three. I never asked him why he'd said that weirdo thing to me, and he never mentioned it either. The last two weeks we had together were really super. Everything went perfectly. And we even decided that he would come up and stay with us for a week. But I didn't tell my parents of the plan for Tony's visit. I figured surprise was the best tactic and anyway he might not be able to make it and then there would be this whole hassle for nothing.

And now here he was.

"What are you doing here? How did you find my room?" I asked, standing close to him, feeling his breath on my cheek.

"I found it 'cause of my picture," he said, looking pleased.

I had his picture on my night table. "Why were you hiding?"

He shrugged. "I thought I'd better since I didn't give any warning. I mean I didn't think your folks would feature seein' me sittin' down in the living room when you got home."

I couldn't believe he was here, in my bedroom. If Dad or Mom should come in . . . well, I could just imagine. I wanted to know everything, but I knew we couldn't go on talking this way. Someone was bound to hear us.

"Let's get out of here," I said. I motioned him to follow me. I opened my door very carefully and peered out. There was no light spilling out from under any of the doors. I prayed they were really all asleep.

"Come on," I whispered.

Carefully we made our way to the stairs and then gingerly crept down them. The creaking was terrible and I was sure everybody would be up in an instant. At every step I imagined my father's booming voice saying: "Who is that?" as he flipped on the light switch.

But nobody heard us. Quickly we made our way to the front door. It was locked, which surprised me. We never locked up. I guess Dad was nervous. I turned the key, and the click it made sounded to me like a crash of cymbals.

Outside we hurried down toward the water. The grass was still wet from the rain and I could feel it on my ankles. The night was cool. I wished I'd brought a jacket. Tony was wearing a sweater over a long-sleeved shirt, so when we got to the water's edge and climbed up on the big rock I asked him for it.

He gave me the sweater and I put it on. For a moment we just sat there staring out at the water. We were on a cove, and the ocean itself was cut off from us by enormous rocks, some of them fifty feet across. Millions of years of waves pounding them had left them smooth, but still they looked, in this light, like prehistoric monsters rising out of the sea.

Finally I turned back toward Tony. He looked as handsome as ever.

"Tell me everything," I said.

He shrugged. "What's to tell? I came to see you."

"Oh, Tony, come on. This isn't how we planned it. Why didn't you let me know so I could've worked on Mom and Dad?"

"It was a sort of the spur-of-the-moment thing."

"What do you mean?"

"I just decided all of a sudden."

"I know what the expression means," I said impatiently. "But how come? What about your job?"

"I quit." He thrust out his chin in a defiant attitude.

"Why?"

"Ah, Anna, I couldn't hack it. My dad has to have everything done just his way."

"Well, it's *his* company."

"Yeah, I know. But he's so damn mean." An expression of sadness filtered through his eyes as if he'd been terribly hurt.

I decided not to push him about the job right then. "When did you get here?" I asked.

"I dunno."

"You don't know what time you got here?"

"I didn't notice."

"Did you come right here, to the house?"

"Yeah."

I felt sick. I knew he was lying. I'd always known whenever Tony lied. He pulled on his left ear. He had

26

no idea he did that and I wasn't going to tell him. Not now, not ever. So he was lying all right. But why?

"Are you sure you came right here?" I wanted to give him another chance to tell the truth.

"Sure I'm sure, what do you mean? Hey, honey," he said, and reached for me.

I moved out of range.

"Hey, what's that? It's been over a month! Don't you love me anymore?"

"Tony," I said, ignoring his question for more reasons than one, "you're lying."

"Well, that's a helluva thing. I come all this way to see you and then you call me a liar. I might as well go." He turned his back to me and put his chin in his hands.

I was beginning to feel frightened. Of Tony? That was dumb, I told myself. Why should I be afraid of Tony? I began to shiver even though I wasn't cold any longer.

"Don't sulk, okay?" I said.

"Why not?"

"Because it's dumb."

"You don't love me," he said.

That was the last thing I wanted to get into.

I said, "Do you know what happened tonight?"

He kept his back to me. "No, what? What do you mean?"

"Look at me," I demanded.

He didn't move. The sound of my heart started thumping in my ears, beating in my throat.

I reached out and touched his arm. "Please, Tony, turn around."

27

Very slowly he did, but he kept his head down, his eyes averted from mine. I took a deep breath.

"A friend of mine was killed tonight . . . murdered."

"YOU'RE KIDDING!" he said.

And I knew he already knew. Tony was a terrible actor, always overdoing it. I waited, staring at him, willing him to look up. Finally he did.

"Okay, Anna, okay," he said. "You always know, don'tcha?"

"Yes," I said. "Now tell me everything."

"I got lousy luck."

What did he mean? I almost told him not to tell me, to go, to run, to leave the island. I don't know what I thought he'd say.

Then he said, "I got to Blue Haven around nine o'clock and I hitched a ride to the restaurant. By the time I got there you guys were just startin' your game. I stayed out of sight."

"Why? Why didn't you let me know you were there?" I wanted to hit him. Maybe if he'd declared himself, things would have been different. Maybe Kirk would be alive. But what did I mean?

"Just wait a minute and I'll tell you, okay?"

"I'm sorry," I said. And I was, for what I'd said and what I'd thought.

"Okay. So I stayed out of sight. See, I knew what you were doin' 'cause you'd written me about the game, remember?"

I nodded.

"Well, I thought it would be neat to find you in the dark when you were hidin', you know, surprise you."

28

"And scare me," I said, annoyed.

A look of guilt crossed his face. "Yeah, that, too."

"So why didn't you?"

"I tried. I couldn't find you. Then there was the whistle and then the scream and I kept hiding out. I don't know why. Then everythin' went haywire."

"You mean when we found . . ."

"Yeah."

"What did you do then?"

"I ran like hell."

"Why?"

"You kiddin' me? Listen, Anna, I was the only stranger there. What do you think would've happened if I'd stayed?"

"But you weren't a stranger to *me*," I said.

"You don't know how people are," he flashed.

"Maybe." We were silent for a moment, and then I said, "Well, what are we going to do now? You can't stay in my closet."

"Yeah, I know. Maybe I could pretend I arrived tomorrow."

"I don't think my parents will be in the mood to see you."

"You mean because of Kirk?"

I sucked in my breath.

"How do you know his name?"

"You told me."

"No I didn't."

"Well, I dunno, I guess I heard someone say it when you found him," he said.

Remembering that moment, I felt a stab of pain. To

blot it out I concentrated on Tony's answer. It sounded logical.

"Okay. So what'll we do?" I asked.

"Look, I want to stay, get a job until I have to go into the Force. We can have our summer just the way we planned it. Hey, Anna, it's gonna be perfect." He reached out then and drew me to him. I felt his lips on mine.

I tried. I really tried. But I didn't feel a thing. I never would have believed it could happen, but it had.

I was a creep.

I had to make it up to him, help him. I thought of the attic. I'd checked it out weeks before, and the part of it that was over my room would be a perfect hiding place. So there was no chance of anyone hearing anything if he moved around. He agreed to stay there until we could figure things out. And I agreed to keep my mouth shut about when he'd arrived.

We went back to the house and I led him upstairs. At the attic door I told him not to open the window in case anyone noticed. I said I'd see him as soon as the coast was clear in the morning.

When I got back to my room I saw that it was ten after three. I crawled under my sheet. I had to get some sleep.

Why had Tony come? And why had he run? I felt frightened. If you didn't do anything, if you were innocent, did you run? Maybe he was lying about not being able to find me. Maybe he'd seen us. If he had—well, then he would have had a motive!

Or had he run because of what he'd said? Would people automatically think he was guilty because he was a stranger? It was probably true that no one would believe any of us had done it if someone they didn't know was handy. But I knew Tony couldn't kill anyone. Could he? No. Never.

5

I awoke with a start, breathless, as if I'd been running. The room was light but not sunny. I rolled over toward the window. The tide was in and I watched as lobster boats, single file in front of our house, made their way out to sea. They would go out past Cole's Light and then part company, each lobsterman going off to haul his own traps.

But even though they separated, they kept in contact with each other by radio. The bigger boats had a stern man but most of the men fished alone, and it was important to be in contact with others in case of squalls or a sudden fog, which was even more dangerous.

I wondered if Watson Hayden was among them. Would he go about his normal routine even though his good friend had been murdered? He might. Maine people, at least the ones on Blue Haven Island, were unusual in a lot of ways. They hardly ever showed emotion, and they seemed to have a "we must go on no matter what" attitude. Watson was the lobsterman (well, he was only eighteen) for our restaurant as well as many others, and I suppose if his traps needed hauling he would have to do it. Still, I couldn't imagine doing anything today, even though I was sure we'd have to open the restaurant because otherwise everything would spoil. Besides, customers counted on us.

Suddenly the reason for not opening, for wondering about Watson, hit me anew. I could feel it like a cement block in the hollow of my stomach. *Kirk was dead.* The three words rang in my ears as if someone else was saying them, loud and long. And yet I couldn't believe it.

If *I* couldn't believe it, what about his parents? And Larry, Nicki and April, his brother and sisters? What did they feel? How was his best friend, Dick Beal, dealing with it? He'd known Kirk all his life. And, of course, Charlotte. Poor Charlotte. It didn't matter what I thought of her—she was his girlfriend; she loved him.

All at once I felt ashamed. What right did I have to mourn Kirk? I'd only known him for five weeks. It seemed to me now that no matter what I'd felt for him in life, my feelings for him in death must be supressed. I was the least important person in this picture, no matter what had happened.

The others were a thousand times closer to Kirk than I. They deserved to cry, to mourn—they'd earned it. Then I remembered. All but one deserved to mourn—one of them had killed Kirk. Unless . . .

Tony! I'd forgotten. He was up in our attic. I looked

at the watch that Dad and Mom had given me for my seventeenth birthday (June eighteenth). It was still too early to go up there. Mom, Dad and Bill left for the restaurant at nine, but Kate and I didn't go over until two in the afternoon. Maybe they *weren't* going to open today.

What would I do? What would Tony do? He couldn't just stay up there indefinitely. He'd starve, die of the heat. I wished now that I hadn't told him not to open a window. Maybe he'd be smart enough, or desperate enough, to open one anyway. He probably would, because Tony usually did what he wanted. Like quitting his job and coming up here unannounced.

Well, if he had to stay up there all day he deserved it. But that was mean. No, I had to find a way to get Tony out of the house, maybe even convince him to go back to New Jersey. I was in no shape to deal with his demands. Besides, after Kirk, Tony seemed like a child. That, I supposed, was mean too. I guess I was just feeling mean today. And why not? I was all mixed up. I'd never loved anyone who'd died before, and I'd never known anyone who was murdered.

A soft, rapping sound made me jump. I sat up and pulled the sheet to my chin.

"Who is it?"

"Bill."

I told him to come in.

He looked tired; his pale skin had dark smudges under his eyes, like blueberry stains. He was wearing a pair of cutoff jeans and an old tie-dyed T-shirt, no shoes. I

34

patted the bed, and he came over and sat down next to me.

"How you doing?" he asked.

"Lousy, how about you?"

"Lousy," he echoed. "You sleep?"

"Not much." I toyed with the idea of telling him about Tony but decided against it. I'd try to handle it myself for now. If I couldn't, I could always call on Bill later. Even though we'd drifted apart a bit, we were still brother and sister and I knew I could count on him in a pinch.

"I hardly slept at all," he said.

"I can't believe what happened. I mean, can you?"

"Who could?" he said. He brought his legs up on the bed and sat in a yoga position, pretzellike. "Anna, I want to ask you something. I mean, it's none of my business but I want to ask you anyway, okay?"

"How can I resist an opening like that?" I said. My heart started going a little faster. Did he know about Tony? Had he heard? Or was it something even worse?

He smiled at me, his brown eyes picking up light from the sun that was now filtering through my window.

"I don't know how to ask," he said.

"Just ask."

"I'm not too hot at stuff like this," he said shyly.

"Like what?" Now I was genuinely confused.

He ran a hand over his hair, pushing it back from his eyes. The red-orangey strands made his skin appear even more pallid than usual. Bill and I never tanned.

"Okay. What I want to know is, were you fooling around with Kirk?"

I could feel the heat creeping up my body from my toes and I knew that I was turning pink. But Bill wasn't looking at me. Embarrassed by his question, he was examining his fingernails and waiting for my answer.

"I'm not sure what you mean," I said. It was only partially true. I knew what he was getting at, but his use of the term "fooling around" wasn't clear. It could have meant many things.

"I mean did you like him?"

"Sure, didn't you?"

"Anna, come on," he said looking up at me. He pressed his lips together in a tight line.

"Well, *didn't* you?" I persisted.

"Give me a break," he said, and shook his head slowly, back and forth. "You think I don't know you just because we haven't exactly been buddies lately. I saw how you looked at him."

Now I felt angry, or maybe scared. At any rate I was defensive. "Well, if you know so much why are you asking me, Bill?"

"I wanted to know for sure." He untangled his feet and jumped off the bed. "Just forget it, okay?"

He started toward the door.

"Oh, Bill," I said, "stop being such a baby."

At the door he turned around. "What's that supposed to mean?"

"All men are alike," I said, thinking of Tony. "You all sulk when you don't get your own way."

"I didn't know you were such an expert on men," he said. He put his hand on the doorknob and opened it.

"Well, there was one man you weren't an expert about—Kirk Cunningham."

He went out and slammed the door behind him before I could ask him what he meant.

I got off the bed and went to my closet. I was beginning to feel sticky in the clothes I'd worn all night. I grabbed a pair of jeans and a polo shirt, some fresh underwear, and headed for the bathroom.

Mom had rigged up a showerlike thing in the big old-fashioned tub. I stepped out of my clothes and got in. The water felt wonderful, cleansing and cool. I stayed there for about twenty minutes, not thinking or feeling but just letting the water roll over me like liquid beads.

When I was dressed in my clean clothes, I went back to my room. Dad was sitting on the end of my bed.

"Hi there, Glamor," he said.

My father is a pretty neat-looking man. Some of my girlfriends back in Maplewood even had crushes on him. Emmy Lou Cahill said she was totally in love with him and would never love anyone else. It's a weird feeling to think your friend is in love with your father.

Anway, I can see that my father's handsome for an older man, but the point is, he *is* an older man. He's real tall, over six feet, and he's very muscular and takes good care of himself. When we lived in Maplewood he was always exercising, doing push-ups and pumping iron and all that sort of thing. But here, with the restaurant, he gets plenty of exercise without doing that stuff. Everybody said it was unusual for somebody who likes to read as much as he does to also be interested in body-building, but I don't see why those things have to be mutually exclusive. People are so into stereotypes.

Dad also has these dreamy brown eyes with very long lashes, and when he cries the lashes get all black and sparkle like they're laced with tiny diamonds. That's how they looked when our dog, Pinter, died last fall.

"Are you going to the restaurant soon?" I asked, trying not to sound too eager.

He looked at me, one eyebrow raised the way he did when he was totally baffled, and I knew the answer before he spoke.

"We're not going to open today, honey. It wouldn't be right."

"But what about the lobsters and steamers and everything?" I asked. "Won't they go bad?"

"We've made arrangements for the food."

"Oh." I waited a few seconds and then said, "And what about the people with reservations?"

"We'll call them, and if we don't get them all one of us will go over to the place at five-thirty and explain." He reached out and took my hand in his. "You're awfully concerned about the restaurant, honey. How come?"

"I don't know. . . . I just . . ." I let the words trail off and shrugged my shoulders.

"Maybe you're focusing your anxiety there instead of where it should be. Are you scared, Glamor?"

"No, I don't think so." I *was* scared, but not of what he meant.

"Good. But if you are don't be afraid to say so, okay?" I nodded.

"Well, look, honey, a detective is here to ask you kids

38

some questions, so you'd better come down, okay?"

I felt my heart skid in my chest. "What kind of questions, Dad?"

"About last night."

"Like in Mom's books?"

"I guess," he said absently. "There's nothing to be afraid of, Anna."

"I'm not afraid, it's just weird."

He stood up. "Yes, I suppose it is. Weird, that is."

"What's he like?" I asked.

"Who?"

"The detective."

"Oh. Well, he seems nice enough. His name is Harvard Smolley." A tiny smile teetered on his lips.

"Harvard Smolley?" I said, almost laughing.

"Harvard Smolley," he repeated, trying to keep from grinning.

"You've gotta be kidding, Dad."

"I kid you not," he said, and put his hand over his heart. "Anyway, we'd better get down there."

"Okay."

Dad put his arm around my shoulder and we left my room together. As we passed the attic door I started to babble very loud about some nonsense, so in case there was any noise up there Dad wouldn't hear anything. I saw him look at me like I was a little crazy and then shake his head. I guess he figured I was upset and he was right. Except he didn't know exactly why.

And I hoped and prayed he wouldn't find out.

6

We sat in the dining room, Detective Smolley across from me at the table. My parents waited in the living room after Dad reluctantly agreed to having me questioned alone.

Detective Smolley was a medium-sized man with light-brown hair and a neatly trimmed mustache. He had large hands and there was a sprinkling of hair across the knuckles. He wore chino pants and a blue short-sleeved shirt, no tie. I'd seen his gun on his right hip when he'd removed his jacket, which was folded over another chair. Now the gun was obscured by the table, but I knew it was there and it made me feel uneasy. I guess I should have felt protected but I didn't. I hate guns no matter who has them.

"Mind if I smoke, deah?" he asked, losing the *r* on dear, the way most of the natives did.

"No."

"I reckon you want one, hmmm?"

"No, thank you. I don't smoke."

"Good girl," he said, and gave me a wink of his blue eye.

I almost laughed. If *he* thought it was such a good thing, why did he smoke? I'll never understand adults.

"Well now, Anna, I'm gonna ask you some questions, some of which you might find unpleasant, if you take my meanin'."

I nodded.

He smiled and it made him look much younger. I figured him for around forty. I smiled back.

"You have real pretty haih," he said.

"Thank you."

"Nice color."

I said nothing.

"You always wear it that way?"

Was this supposed to be the kind of question that I was going to find unpleasant? I wondered. If it was, I didn't. "Not always." My hair was straight and, like today, I usually wore it parted in the middle and hanging loose. It came to below my shoulders.

"What other ways do you wear it, deah?"

"In a ponytail."

"When?"

"When what?"

"When do you wear it that way? In the ponytail?"

This was really dumb. What did how I wore my hair have to do with anything? "I don't know. Well, I wear it back when I'm working at the restaurant, you know, so it won't get in the food or anything."

41

"Ay-uh. So then I reckon you wore it in a ponytail last night, that right?"

"You mean at work?"

He nodded.

"Sure. I always do."

"How about after work?" He blew a puff of smoke through rounded lips and made a ring.

Watching it float upward, I said, "No, I take it down after work." Then I stopped and thought. "Wait a minute."

"Yes?"

"I didn't last night. I left it the way it was."

"Why's that?"

"Why do you want to know?"

He smiled. "Just curious."

I didn't believe that one for a second. But I didn't argue the point. Let him think I was some nerd who would buy that. "I left it the way it was because it was sort of hot last night." And because we were going to play the game, I thought. But I didn't say that. I guess I didn't want to talk about the game before I had to.

"Well," he said, "it's real pretty haih."

"Thanks."

"Now then, why don't you tell me about the Cunninghams."

I felt a clutch inside, like a hand grabbing me. I don't know why. Maybe it was just the whole situation. I'd read so many mysteries in my life, my mother's and others, and that was a whole different thing. Detectives grilling people in books is fun to read, but this wasn't fun. This was real life. And there was also the matter of Tony in the attic. Should I tell Smolley that he was up there? If I did, my parents would find out and I'd probably be grounded for weeks. But I'd been taught to always respect the law. Still, my loyalty was to Tony even though I didn't feel the way I used to about him. I was thoroughly confused.

"The Cunninghams," Smolley prompted.

"What do you want to know about them?"

"Oh, anythin' 'tall, everythin'." He gave the boyish smile again.

I didn't know where to start and told him so.

"Well, now, you and your family are from away, so how about tellin' me about your meetin' with them. When was that?"

"About five weeks ago." I could hardly believe it. I felt as if I'd known them all my life. But I hadn't.

The first night we were on Blue Haven Island, after we finished unloading the truck, we were told we were going to the Cunninghams' to dinner and that they were the people Mom and Dad had bought the restaurant from. I remember that none of us kids wanted to go. We thought it would be a drag hanging around with old people all evening, and Mom just smiled and said she'd bet us each fifty cents that when it was time to go we wouldn't want to leave. Bill had said not to bet, that it was a trap, but Kate and I did anyway.

And when we walked in the door I was ready to collect my fifty cents from Mom. Lloyd Cunningham was definitely around fifty, with sparse gray hair that stuck out in wisps from under a red baseball cap. He wasn't fat but he was stocky and there were dark circles under his eyes. Ella Cunningham was about the same age, but her hair was black and curly with only a few streaks of gray. She seemed to be a jolly type, but there was something unreal about it, something forced. And there was a look of sadness in her eyes that told me what I saw on the surface wasn't the whole story. Still, the Cunninghams seemed nice, very friendly and warm, but even so it looked like a snore-o for the evening.

And then I saw him!

He was coming down the twisting staircase, his blond hair flopping casually over one eye. Talk about your movie stars. I'd never seen such piercing blue eyes. He wore jeans and a green T-shirt and on his feet were tassel loafers with no socks.

Behind him came another guy about the same age but he was definitely not your movie-star type. In fact, he was almost funny-looking. But maybe it was the contrast. This one was shorter than the other one and had muddy brown hair that hung limply, like old spaghetti. His nose was too big and his eyes too small. He was wearing faded jeans and a gray sweat shirt. His sneakers had holes in them.

"This is our son, Kirk," Mr. Cunningham said, pointing to the gorgeous one, "and his friend Dick Beal. *Our* friend, I should say. We've known Dick since he was in diapers." He patted Dick on the back and Dick smiled, showing even white teeth. They perked up his looks a lot. We were all introduced and Kirk was especially warm to Bill. Kirk wasn't super tall, maybe around five eleven, and most guys that size really try to lord it over Bill by squaring their shoulders and making themselves look

44

taller. But Kirk, I noticed, kind of slumped down. It was very subtle and I don't think Bill caught on, but I was always aware of how guys acted around him. That was one of the things I liked about Tony. He never tried to puff himself up around Bill.

"It's nice to meet all of you," Kirk said, grinning. It was the kind of smile that takes you by surprise and turns your stomach upside down. I glanced at Mom, and she had her right hand near her hip, palm up waiting for the fifty cents we'd bet. I looked away, trying not to laugh.

Dick Beal stuck his hand out for my dad to take and then did the same to Bill. It's funny the way guys never want to shake hands with girls. I like to shake hands because you can tell a lot about a person that way. I put my hand out and Dick hesitated only a beat before taking it. It was a nice firm shake. I decided I liked him.

Seeing this, Kirk went around shaking hands with all of us, and when he came to me he gave that smile. I felt my knees tremble and I didn't dare look at Mom. His handshake disappointed me a little. It was almost limp. I told myself he just didn't want to hurt me so he was taking it easy.

Dick said, "Will you be opening the restaurant soon, Mr. Parker?"

"End of the week. Why?"

"Well, I'd like to work for you. I've worked for the Cunninghams ever since they opened the clambake." Dick pushed his stringy hair back off his forehead.

"We'd be happy to have you with us then."

"Thanks," Dick said, and smiled awkwardly. For a

second I thought he was trying to imitate Kirk's smile. If he was, he failed.

I wondered if Kirk was going to work at the restaurant too, but I didn't know how to find out without asking directly and I thought that might look too obvious. Maybe Dad would ask, I thought. But he didn't get the chance.

Kirk said, "I'm real sorry we can't stay but we have previous plans." And then they were gone.

"So, then, Anna," Detective Smolley said, "you didn't get to know those fellas the first night."

"No, not until later," I said.

"Where were they goin' that night? Do you recollect?"

How could I forget? "He had a date with his girl-friend, Charlotte Coombs."

"And Mr. Beal?"

"He was going with them. To the movies."

Smolley raised an eyebrow in a perfect arch.

"That's the way Kirk was," I said, feeling his loss all over again at the word *was*. "He let Dick tag along. They were best friends."

"Pretty darn generous. Leastways it seems like it to me."

"Yes, generous," I said.

"So, Anna, do you know her?"

"Who?"

"This here Charlotte Coombs."

"Oh, her. Sure. She works at the restaurant."

"Do you like her?"

The question took me by surprise. I was dreading the thought of talking about Charlotte, but I didn't think he was going to ask if I *liked* her.

46

"Somethin' wrong?" he asked.

"No, nothing."

"You don't like her," he said perceptively.

"She's okay." It wasn't fair to ask me to give an opinion about Charlotte, but I couldn't tell him that. In my opinion she was dumb, selfish and babyish. But what did I know? Still, I wasn't alone. I remembered that first night when Larry Cunningham said:

"She's a pain in the tail."

I looked at his sister, Nicki, for confirmation.

"Charlotte's okay," she said. "She's just kind of, I don't know, wimpy, I guess."

"You guess?" Larry said. "She is a wimp with a capital W. The only thing that Froot Loop will eat is green beans, hamburger and mashed potatoes. Then she puts ketchup all over them and mixes it up. Gag me!" he said, and held his stomach.

I realized that Detective Smolley would be asking the others what they thought of Charlotte, so it wouldn't look too weird if I told the truth. But my truth was different from theirs. Well, he wouldn't know that.

"She's sort of a wimp."

"How's that?"

"I don't know. A wimp's a wimp."

"Is Dick Beal a wimp?"

"No, he's a neat guy," I said. And he was. He was kind and considerate and always helpful.

"Ay-uh. Let's go back to the other Cunninghams and when you met them."

"Okay."

There were three others: Larry, Nicole and April.

Larry was my age. He was one of those goofy-looking guys who wore his pants somewhere up around the middle of his chest and the next-to-top button of his shirt closed. But he was a decent boy.

Nicole, who told us to call her Nicki, was as pretty as Kirk was handsome. She had the same blond hair and the same piercing blue eyes. She was sixteen, and even though she was younger than I, that night I felt awkward and strange around her. I don't know why, but sometimes I feel more nervous about meeting girls than I do boys. I think girls are harder on each other. We're always judging and comparing. And as it turned out, Nicki didn't take to me at all. I don't know why. I wanted to be friends with her but she kept to herself, inside an invisible shell, and I just couldn't crack it. It's been a big disappointment and made me miss Kristen even more than I would have.

April was twelve, with her mother's black, curly hair and brown eyes. She and Kate hit it off immediately and went up to April's room to look at April's collection of stickers, something Kate was very into.

Our parents all had cocktails and the four of us went down into their basement, which was fixed up with a bar, a jukebox, Ping-Pong, darts, stereo and television. We spent the first fifteen minutes finding out our Vital Statistics and then got down to the grittier stuff.

I asked the all-important question. "What's this restaurant like?"

"It's not like anything you've ever been to, I'll bet," Larry said.

"Yeah, but what's it like?"

"When you think of a restaurant, what do you think of?"

I shrugged. "I don't know. A room with tables and chairs and stuff."

"Tablecloths and candles, silver, china, roses in vases, right?" he asked, grinning.

"I guess."

Bill said, "Or Formica tables with ketchup bottles and little tubs of mustard. It's all lit with fluorescent lights and the smell of grease is just hanging in the air ready to glom onto all your clothes. Yuck."

"Dis-gusting," said Nicki, smiling and looking interested in the conversation for the first time.

"Well," Larry said, "our restaurant—or should I say . . . your restaurant—isn't like either of those."

"It's not?" I said nervously.

"Nope. It's got no walls, no ceiling, no real floor."

"Give me a break," Bill said.

"No kidding. The floor is the grass and the ceiling's the sky."

"And the tables are trees," I said, joking.

Larry said, "In a way. The tables are long, wooden picnic jobs and the chairs benches. Everybody just sits with everybody, family style."

The whole thing was sounding weirder and weirder. I glanced at Bill and he raised his eyebrows, his mouth screwed over to one side in bewilderment.

"So what about the food?" he asked.

Nicki said, "The price is the same for everyone: fifteen bucks. For that you get as many steamers as you can eat; a pound-and-a-quarter lobster; two ears of corn, coffee, beer or soda; and dessert, which is blueberry pie. Oh, yeah, you get butter and plenty of napkins, too."

"Sounds great." I was ready to eat the whole thing right then.

"It is great," Larry said. "That's the good news."

"And the bad news?" I asked.

"*We* cook it."

"Gotcha," I said. "Well, do you broil the lobsters or what?"

"Nicki and Larry laughed. I felt like a jerk.

"Sorry," Larry said. "No, we don't broil them or boil them or fry them."

"Fried lobster," Bill said, "sounds good." He rubbed his belly.

"Mmmm, delicious," Nicki said, rubbing *her* belly. "And baked steamers, mmmmm."

"Sauteed corn on the cob," Bill added.

I didn't really feel like getting into it because I wanted to know more about the restaurant, but I also didn't want to seem like a grouch so I added my two cents.

"Roasted blueberry pie. Yum." They all laughed, and when it died down a bit I said, "Seriously, Larry, how do you cook the lobsters?"

"Well, everything is cooked in these huge pits in the ground. The bottoms of the pits are lined with driftwood and then we start a fire. That's done early in the day."

Nicki went on, "Then when that's good and hot we put these humongous rocks on top of the fire and then seaweed on top of them."

"Seaweed that one of us has collected," Larry said.

"Pain in the butt." He twirled a piece of his black hair around a finger.

"Anyway," Nicki continued, "the lobsters, steamers and corn are laid across the seaweed and rocks, and then a wet tarpaulin goes over the whole thing to keep the heat from escaping."

"It sounds neat," I said.

"Neat to eat," said Larry, "but hard work."

My heart sank. "Really hard?"

"Really."

"I guess you guys are glad to be out of it then, huh?"

"Oh, we're not out of it," Larry said. "We'll be working right alongside you."

"How come?" Bill asked.

"Didn't your parents tell you anything?" Nicki asked.

Bill and I shook our heads.

"Well," she went on, "one of the conditions of the sale was that we would all continue working. All us kids, that is. I guess Mom and Dad will be around a bit in the beginning, but then . . . then they won't."

She had a funny look on her face and I thought for a second she might cry, then I was sure I'd imagined it.

"But you two and Kirk will be there?" I asked, trying to sound as casual as possible.

Nicki wasn't fooled for a minute. "Kirk will be there," she said, sounding a little disgusted.

I pretended not to notice her tone. Some girls don't like their friends to be interested in their brothers. Maybe Nicki was one of them. I'd play it very cool. "So does this restaurant make any money?" I asked.

51

"It does okay," Larry said.

"Last year Larry saved about five hundred dollars. But don't get excited, he's the cheapest guy in town. He never spends a cent," Nicki said.

"Not true. I bought my Apple, didn't I?"

"Apple?" Bill said, his face lighting up.

Even I knew an Apple was a computer.

"Yeah, sure. You into computers?"

"I have a Kaypro."

"No kidding?"

"Oh, bore," Nicki said, rolling her eyes at me.

I smiled meekly, but I couldn't really get into it with her, because Bill knew that I liked the computer and was always begging for time on it before it was taken away from him as punishment for his theft. Lots of girls are afraid of them, but I think they're fun. Anyway, I guess that didn't endear me to Nicki either.

"I'll show it to you after dinner, Bill," Larry said.

"Sure," Bill said. "Whatever."

Then, by accident, I asked the key question.

"How come your parents sold the restaurant if it's such a great thing?"

Larry and Nicki looked at each other and nodded.

"I guess you might as well know," she said. "It's because my dad's sick. He has a brain tumor."

"Gee," I said stupidly, "he doesn't look sick."

"You don't always look that sick with a brain tumor," Larry said. "And you don't lose weight like with other cancers."

"Is he in a lot of pain?" Bill asked.

"No. Only when he has his treatments."

I realized now that that must have been why Mr. Cunningham was wearing the baseball cap, to hide the radiation marks. And this also explained what I'd seen in Mrs. Cunningham's eyes and why she was pushing happiness. I'd never known anyone with a brain tumor, but I knew it was pretty awful.

"Is he going to have an operation?" I asked.

"No. They can't operate."

Nobody said anything then. We all just sat there, staring at the floor. I thought I knew what was going to happen to Mr. Cunningham but I couldn't be sure. I wanted to ask but I was afraid.

Nicki told us anyway. "He's going to die," she said, and her eyes filled.

"When?" I asked before I could stop myself.

She shrugged and some tears trickled down her cheeks.

Larry said, "We can't be sure, but maybe not until the end of the summer."

Sometimes I thought Nicki's aloofness with me was because of her father dying, but then I noticed she wasn't that way with Bill or the others. I had to accept that she just didn't like me.

Should I, I wondered, mention to Detective Smolley that Mr. Cunningham was sick, was going to die? I figured he probably knew it anyway. Everybody seemed to know everybody's business on Blue Haven Island. Besides, Mr. Cunningham had taken a very bad turn a week ago and his right arm and leg were paralyzed. I hadn't seen him, but Larry told me he looked just awful and was either in a wheelchair or in bed.

I just couldn't imagine what it would be like if Dad

got sick and was going to die. I don't know if I could be as brave as the Cunningham kids. And now they'd lost their brother, too. It was really tragic.

"So you like all the Cunninghams then?" Detective Smolley asked.

"Yes. All of them." There was no point in going into the thing about Nicki because I wasn't really lying. I wanted to like her and I would have if she'd let me.

Smolley took another cigarette from his pack, lit it and blew a plume of smoke above our heads. And then he said the words I didn't want to hear but knew I'd have to. "Okay, then. Let's talk about the deceased."

It made me feel sick.

7

The first day at the restaurant I was nervous and scared and I kept getting things all bollixed up. Kirk kept telling me to take it easy, relax. But I couldn't relax because of him. Every time he accidentally touched my hand or brushed against me, my knees shook and my stomach whirled around as if it had a life of its own. I think Charlotte knew that I was interested in Kirk, because she was nasty to me from the start.

"Looks like you have two left feet, kid," she said when I tripped over a lobster crate.

"Don't pay any attention to her," Kirk said when Charlotte was out of hearing range. "She's a drag."

It surprised me that he'd say that about his girlfriend, but I figured he was trying to make me feel better.

"You're doing just fine," he went on. "My first day here I put the lobsters on *top* of the tarpaulin." He laughed and I laughed with him. "Boy, did I ever feel like a jerk when I did it the other way. So don't mind Charlotte. She probably put the tarpaulin on her head the first day."

We laughed together again and I was particularly struck by the light in his eyes—the light of life.

And now he was dead. I couldn't believe it.

"Did you like Kirk, Anna?" the detective asked.

I swallowed and blinked back tears. "Yes," I whispered.

"You can cry, gal," he said.

"I'm okay." For some reason I didn't want to cry in front of Detective Smolley.

"You sure?"

"Sure."

"Good."

Now I knew why. He really didn't want me to cry. I was "good" if I didn't cry.

"Was there anyone, would you calculate, who didn't like Kirk?"

"Everybody liked him."

"Somebody didn't."

"Well, maybe it wasn't one of the kids. Maybe it was just some drifter in the woods."

"Mebbe," he said.

"Well, why are you so intent on blaming one of us?"

"I didn't say I was."

That was true, he hadn't. I was the one who thought that. I felt trapped. "You just seemed, well, I don't know, like maybe you thought one of us did it."

"Mebbe one of you did. But then again, like you point

out, it's a possibility that it was an outsider. Someone who wasn't in the game but was in the woods . . . waitin'," he said ominously.

I immediately thought of Tony. Was I doing a terrible thing by not telling about him? No. Tony was innocent. Besides, if anything happened to make me think differently I could tell Smolley later.

"Was Kirk your boyfriend?"

"No," I said quickly. "I told you, Charlotte was Kirk's girlfriend."

"Ay-uh, that's right. You told me that." He stubbed out his cigarette. "But you liked Kirk a lot, didn't you?"

I didn't know what to say. What point would it serve if I told the truth now? I was starting to feel guilty about keeping all these secrets, but I felt that what Kirk and I had together had nothing to do with his murder.

"I liked Kirk a lot, yes," I said. "But no more or less than any of the others."

"Ay-uh," he mumbled. Then he reached over to his jacket, pulled something from the pocket and laid it on the table.

It was a knife in a plastic bag. My heart gave a lurch.

"You recognize that?" he asked.

I nodded.

"Whose is it?"

"Kirk's," I said.

"You know where I got it?"

Tears sprang up behind my eyes.

Smolley reached across the table and patted my hand. "Now, now, deah, I don't mean to upset you but I gotta ask."

57

"I know. It's . . . it's the one . . . it's the one that killed Kirk," I said finally.

"That's right. When's the last time you saw it?"

I felt dizzy, thought I might faint and grabbed the table edge with both hands. The last time I'd seen the knife it had been sticking out of Kirk's back.

Smolley read my mind. "Before that," he said kindly.

I took a deep breath. "I can't remember," I lied. "He always carried it in his pocket."

"Ay-uh." He put the knife back in his jacket, then looked at me for a long moment. "Those are pretty earrin's," he said.

"Thank you."

"My daughter wants to have her eahs pierced, but I've been sayin' no. How come both earrin's in one ear?"

"That's the style."

"Your parents didn't mind?"

"No," I lied again.

As a going-away present Kristen gave me these two stud earrings with little red stones in them, so what else could I do? Nobody I know pierces both ears and some people even triple pierce one ear. But the thing is that my parents had told me months before that they didn't want me to, not even one in each ear. I don't know what made me do it—I knew they'd freak over it. Maybe that's why!

I waited until the day before we moved and then I just went to the jewelry store in town and the woman there shot the studs through my earlobe with this little gunlike instrument. *Bam! Bam!* and it was over. It didn't even hurt. Well, it stung, a little. Since I wear my hair over my ears it wasn't until the morning of the move that Mom noticed. She'd come in to wake me and my hair was away from my face, so the first words I heard her say were:

"You little creep!"

Fortunately there was too much to do that morning so nothing more was said, and once we got here she just let it drop. Every once in a while, when my hair is tied back, I catch her staring at my ear and then she shakes her head disapprovingly.

"I reckon I should let Bahbra, that's my daughta, get hers pierced."

I didn't say anything because I honestly didn't care whether Barbara got her ears pierced or not.

"Tell me about Watson Hayden," Detective Smolley said.

I think he talked about pierced ears and hair and things like that just to get me off-balance. It worked.

"Anna," he said softly, "did you heah me?"

"Yes."

"Watson Hayden," he reminded.

"He's our lobsterman. He catches them and we buy them from him."

"How old is Watson?"

"Eighteen. He just graduated from high school. He's not going to college," I said sadly.

"Should he go to college?"

"Kirk says he's very smart, but Watson's dad wants him to stay here and keep working with him. There's a lot of kids in the family—eight, I think—and they need the money."

"Is Watson mad about that?"

"Wouldn't you be if you wanted to go to college?"

"I don't know. I never wanted to go. Is Watson?"

"I guess so . . . yes . . . he is."

"How do you know?"

Kirk had told me but I didn't want to say that. "Everybody knows," I said instead.

"Ay-uh."

It seemed Detective Smolley was always saying *ay-uh*. I wondered if it was when he believed something or when he didn't.

"Who else in the group?"

"Dick Beal."

"Kirk's best friend," Smolley said.

"Yes."

"And that was it. There was no one else around last night?"

Again I thought of Tony and my heart gave an extra thump. "No one," I said.

"Youh sure?" Smoke curled around his head like a question mark.

I looked at his nose the way Kristen had taught me. "If you're lying," she said, "always look at their noses, never into their eyes. It appears the same but they can't tell you're lying."

"Yes, I'm sure," I said, guilt wrapping around me like a heavy cloak.

"Ay-uh."

There it was again and now I knew he didn't believe me. So what? He couldn't prove anything, and anyway Tony hadn't killed Kirk. He didn't even know him. His

60

arrival last night was coincidence. I hoped he was okay up there in the attic. He must have been hungry by now.

"Tell me about the game?" Smolley asked.

Wham! Like that. *Tell me about the game.*

"It's not like Dungeons and Dragons," I said defensively. Everybody knew that that could be a dangerous game.

"What *is* it like?"

"It's just a game."

"Anna, if you don't tell me somebody else will."

So why didn't he ask somebody else? Why me?

"Am I the first person you've talked to?"

"Ay-uh," he said.

"Why did you pick me?"

"No reason, just chance."

"Ay-uh," I said. *I* didn't believe *him.*

"Are you scairt to tell me about the game?" he asked.

"No." But I was. I don't know why. It wasn't the game in itself. A game is a game. But after what happened I guess I was afraid of it sounding bad. Still, we played it over and over and nothing had ever gone wrong before. *Gone wrong!* Who was I kidding? Murder is a lot more than something going wrong.

"What do you call the game?" he asked.

I looked at him. His blue eyes told me nothing. But a twitching muscle in his right cheek said everything. Detective Smolley wasn't as relaxed as he pretended to be. I knew he knew what the game was called, so why was he doing this? Was Smolley a sadist?

"You know," I said.

"No, I don't."

I shot it at him. "Murder. The game is called Murder."

He didn't blink an eye but the cheek gave an extra twitch.

"So how do you play it?" he asked.

I took a deep breath and wiped my sweating palms on my shorts. "The rules? You mean you want the rules?"

"That's right."

My mind felt like mush. I couldn't put any thoughts together.

"Anna, did you heah me?"

"I heard. You want the rules. Okay." I closed my eyes for a second and tried to clear my head of anything but the game. "Okay," I said again. "I'll tell you."

"Good." He touched a hairy finger to his mustache, smoothing it down.

"Let's say there are ten people in the game and . . ."

"How many in the game last night?"

I calculated quickly in my head. "Eight."

"Then let's say eight in the game."

"All right. Eight. So then you have eight pieces of paper."

"What kind of paper?"

"Any kind."

"What kind you have last night?"

This was really dumb. What difference did it make? "Yellow lined paper." I anticipated his next question. "We get it from the office inside the cabin. At the restaurant."

"Go on." He smiled but this time he looked old. Maybe he was tired of me.

"So there are these eight pieces of paper and one is

marked with a D for detective and one M for murderer. The rest are blank."

"Who marks them?"

"Anyone."

"Who marked them last night?"

It was totally stupid but I felt scared. "I did." Marking the papers had nothing to do with anything.

He nodded. "Then what do you do?"

"We fold the papers up in little squares and throw them in a bowl or bucket or whatever's handy. Then we each pick one." I was beginning to breathe in a shallow way, like I was hyperventilating. Anxiety.

"And then?"

"Then each person picks a piece of paper. Everyone opens them up. The detective, the one who gets D, says so right away. The rest, the one who gets M and the others who get blanks, say nothing."

"Why does the detective declare himself?"

"I was just going to tell you," I said, annoyed.

"Sorry. Go ahead." He lit another cigarette.

"The detective is the one who times everything and blows the whistle." I put up my hand to stop him as he opened his mouth. "When the detective says *go*, everybody runs to hide and he times three minutes until he blows the whistle. The murderer has three more minutes to find his victim. There's a second whistle. Then the murderer taps the victim and says, 'I'm the murderer' or 'You're dead' or some dumb thing like that. So the victim screams and everybody runs back to where we started. But not right away."

"Meanin'?"

"Part of the fun is for everybody to try and fool the detective, so you take your time going back to home base after the scream. People straggle in at different times."

"The victim, too?"

"No. The victim stays where he or she is. We all go looking, find the victim and then bring the 'corpse' back in."

"Is that it? Is that the game?" he asked.

I really wondered how smart this Smolley was. I mean, who would play such a tacky game if that's all it was?

"This is a game of deduction," I said, sitting up straighter in my chair.

"How's that done?"

"The detective asks everybody except the victim questions about their whereabouts and what they saw and heard. Only the murderer can lie. So then the detective has two guesses and that's it."

He stubbed out his cigarette and stood up.

"Well, now, thank you, Anna, you've been real helpful."

I watched in amazement as he put on his jacket. Didn't he want to know about last night? What I heard and saw? Didn't he care who was the detective, who was the murderer? What kind of cop was he?

"Is that all?"

"For now," he said.

I was very relieved.

He walked out into the living room and I followed. Dad stood up as we came into the room.

"Everything go all right?" he asked, sounding nervous.

"Just fine," Smolley said. "Anna was real helpful. Now I'd like to talk to Bill."

Bill was sitting at the piano, his back to it. He looked scared. I wanted to tell him there was nothing to be afraid of, but I didn't see how to do it with all the adults around. Just then he glanced my way and I gave him a wink, first with one eye and then the other. It was something we'd done when we were little to say that everything was okay. He caught the winks and I thought I saw him relax a little.

"Would you come in here with me, son?" Detective Smolley said.

They disappeared into the dining room. Dad put his arm around me and gave me a hug.

"You okay, Glamor?"

"Sure," I said, throwing him a big smile.

Mom stroked my hair. "I'm sorry you have to go through this, darling."

"It's okay," I said. "I think I'll go up and lie down." I wanted to get to Tony. "Are you going out?"

"When the detective goes we're going to the store," Mom said. "Do you mind being left alone?"

I had to keep myself from shouting with joy. "No, don't worry about me. I'm fine. Honest." I went upstairs.

All I could do now was wait until the detective and Mom and Dad left the house. I couldn't hurry time and I couldn't make anyone disappear. I'd just have to wait, and unfortunately, so would Tony.

I wondered if Smolley would ask Bill the same questions he'd asked me. Would he ask him about last night's game, go further and ask the things he *didn't* ask me?

Like who was the detective and who was the murderer? And if he did, what would Bill say? He would tell the truth, I guessed, as I would have done. But he only knew part of it. Like everyone else, he only knew that Larry was the detective. When we'd found Kirk, that had ended the game. No one bothered to ask or cared who the murderer was. But I knew.

It was me.

8

I didn't mean for anything to start up between me and Kirk. But there's no denying that I liked him from the beginning. That first night I kept thinking about him and thinking about him way into the small hours of the morning. The next day I was a wreck. I remember my mom asking me why I looked so tired.

"Are you so upset to be here, Anna?"

Having met Kirk was already making Blue Haven Island more interesting. "No," I said, "I'm accepting it." I didn't want to give in to her too easily. It had already cost me fifty cents!

"Well, you look like you didn't sleep at all."

"I slept," I said. I wished she were writing a book, because when she did she was a lot less focused on me.

The thing is Mom has Libby Crawford to think about. Libby is her fictional detective, and when Mom's writing a novel she gets all involved and everything else just sort of goes by the wayside. I don't mean that she completely ignores us or stops loving us or anything. It's just that she isn't quite so conscious of what we kids are doing every minute. See, Mom is really interested in us: our grades, our friends and what we think, which is neat. But sometimes it's nice to sort of be on your own. It's what I mean about the focus. When Mom is concentrating on Libby, then I can do pretty much what I please. I don't mean staying out all night or stuff like that, but the emphasis shifts and for the six months that she's writing a book I don't feel as though I'm being scrutinized like a specimen on a slide.

Well, anyway, since she wasn't writing, that morning she just kept bugging me, asking millions of questions as to why I looked so crummy, which made me feel a hundred percent crummier.

And then she started in on Kirk.

"What did you think of the Cunningham boy? Handsome, isn't he?"

"Larry?" I said, just for fun.

"Larry? No, of course not. The other one, Kirk."

"Oh, him," I said, very cool. "I didn't notice."

"That, my dear, is an out-and-out lie. You noticed all right. What an improvement he'd be over Tony."

"Please don't start on Tony," I pleaded.

"Don't worry. The less said about him the better. Thank God he's out of your life."

I said nothing.

"Oh, I know you'll get letters from him, but letters don't worry me."

"Will you read them?" I asked.

Her big green eyes got bigger and her mouth opened into a little O.

"I just wondered," I said casually.

"Anna, I know you think I'm a huge pain, but I'm not immoral. I would *never* read your mail."

"Well, I know you *love* mail."

You see, my mother is a mail freak! She writes to everyone. Newspapers, radio and television people, other writers, mayors, members of congress, senators and even the president. Most of these letters are complaints; some are complimentary. She does it because she loves getting the answers. She's freaky over mail.

"I admit I like getting mail, but I only like getting mail that's mine. I'm not interested in yours, Anna."

"I noticed that you bought the local paper this morning. Are you going to start writing letters to the editor here, too?"

"What's it to you, kid?" she asked, trying to sound like Humphrey Bogart.

"I don't think it's a hot idea, that's all."

"Oh, no? Why not?"

"You're a businesswoman now."

"So?"

"Your letters might antagonize some people—like customers. I mean, if they get printed in the paper," I said.

She looked at me, into my eyes the way she did sometimes, as if she was looking into my soul. Then she laughed and kind of shook her head back and forth like she'd just discovered the secret to eternal life or something.

"You're cute," she said, "you really are."

"Why, thank you," I said, playing it straight.

"It's you you're thinking of, isn't it?"

"I don't know what you mean." But of course I did.

And then she reached out and put both her hands on my shoulders. "Seriously, Anna, does my letter writing bother you?"

I shrugged.

"Tell me, honey."

"Well, sometimes," I admitted.

"When?" She looked upset now.

"It doesn't matter."

"Sure it does. Your feelings always matter to me."

"Really?"

She looked astonished. "Of course they do. Do you think I don't have respect for your feelings?"

"Well, I know you love me and all, but I didn't think you cared what I felt about stuff *you* do."

"Well, I do." She slipped an arm around my shoulder and guided me to the wicker couch, where we sat down. "I wouldn't want to ever do anything that would embarrass you, Anna."

I was starting to feel bad about this conversation. I wasn't into making my mother feel rotten, because she is basically a terrific person. I mean, maybe she's a little eccentric, but that's what makes her interesting. She isn't like just any old run-of-the-mill mother. On the other hand having a different kind of mother can be a setup for humiliations now and then. Still, I wouldn't have wanted anyone else to be my mother.

"Let's just forget it," I said.

70

"No. I want you to tell me what you're feeling."

"Okay, if you really mean it."

"I do."

"Well, like I said, I think writing letters to the local paper might not be such a great idea."

She deliberated for a moment or two and then she said, "You might be right."

I brightened. "You think?"

"I guess you have a point about me being a business-woman and that my letters might have an adverse effect on the restaurant."

"No kidding, you really think so?"

"Yes. I promise that I won't write to any papers within a hundred-mile radius."

She smiled but I didn't.

"Okay," she said, "two hundred."

Now I smiled. "Thanks, Mom."

"Anytime. So where were we?" she asked. "Oh, I remember. We were talking about Kirk."

In fact we'd been talking about Tony, but I let it pass.

"Do you happen to know if his date was somebody special?" she asked me.

"Only his girlfriend," I said.

"Oh."

And that was the end of that particular conversation. But it didn't stop me from thinking and dreaming. Dreams are harmless and I've always indulged myself in them. I was very proficient at daydreaming, often to the consternation of my teachers. There were no boundaries for my dreaming: school, football games, dates . . . I'd do it anywhere.

71

I was sure then that anything I was going to have with Kirk Cunningham was going to be in dreams, because one thing I'd decided a long time ago that I'd never do was to try and steal another girl's boyfriend.

And even after I met Charlotte and saw what a pain she was, it didn't change my ideas about that. A person has to have principles.

But almost right away Kirk made it very hard to stick to my guns. He was so neat. Really nice to me, making me feel comfortable and wanted. Something that Nicki and Charlotte didn't do at all.

And then at the end of the first week, Charlotte was sick and didn't come to work, so Kirk asked me if I wanted to collect the driftwood with him.

When we walked down the beach together Nicki gave me a dirty look, but I didn't care. What was I doing, after all? Collecting driftwood. Big deal. Still, I guess somewhere I knew it was more than that, or would be. But I had no intention of not going with him, even though I felt a streak of guilt shoot through me.

This particular stretch of beach was not at all like the one in front of our cottage. There were no big monster rocks in the water. But it had secret deep-water coves with golden sand. Back near where we'd come down there were dark mossy forests and granite hilltops. And as we walked along, silently, we found driftwood and flotsam lying above the tide line.

I couldn't think of anything to say, so I just kept walking and picking up the wood, piling it into a basket. Finally the basket became too heavy for me to carry any more. I had to stop.

"I think I'd better take this back, Kirk," I said.

"Let's sit a minute. They won't miss us."

I won't deny that I was elated. I wanted very much to be with him alone, and since Charlotte was sick this might be my only chance. I never thought anything more would come of it. But right away, as we sat there looking out at the water, which looked like a great bowl of blue light, he changed everything.

"I'm really glad to be alone with you, Anna."

I didn't know what to say. So I said nothing and just kept looking at the bay. And then I felt his fingers under my chin as he turned my head to look at him.

"Did you hear me?" he asked.

"Yes," I whispered.

"How about you? Are you glad to be alone with me?"

Should I lie? I couldn't. "Yes, I am."

He smiled that wonderful way and I almost felt dizzy. He dropped his hand from my chin and slid it down my arm to my hand, where he left it, covering mine. Neither of us said anything more. We just looked into each other's eyes. I felt as if I was in a trance and then I heard our names being called.

It was Nicki.

"Hey, you guys," she said, "we need the wood."

So we went back.

That was the first time but it didn't stop there. Whenever he could, Kirk found time to be alone with me. And I did nothing to discourage him. I couldn't help myself. I'm not trying to make excuses, but it was almost like I was under a spell, as if I didn't have any control over what I did where Kirk was concerned.

73

In our stolen moments we whispered sweet things to each other and we held hands and kissed. But still, he went on seeing Charlotte and I felt awful. Even so I couldn't find it in me to tell him to leave me alone.

At the beginning of the last week Kirk was alive, I decided to try and make a demand. I was feeling too awful about Charlotte and myself and I told him so.

"What would you like me to do?" he asked.

"I guess I want you to break up with Charlotte," I said.

"Or what?"

"What do you mean?"

"Or you won't be with me anymore? Is that it?" he asked, looking very sad.

I knew I couldn't threaten him with that, because I'd never be able to stick to it.

"No," I said, "I don't believe in threats."

"You're a wonderful girl, Anna. So much more mature than Charlotte. But she's so delicate. She had a nervous breakdown once, did you know that?"

"No. Really?"

He nodded.

"So you're afraid then to tell her, for fear she'll break down again, is that it?" I asked.

"That's it."

"Then don't," I said.

"No, I have to. I have to sometime, don't I? Why not now, when I've found someone as wonderful as you? I'll tell her tonight."

But he didn't. Not that night or any of the nights that followed. Then the day of the murder he surprised me.

I was sitting on the porch of our house waiting for Kate to come up from the beach so we could go to the restaurant when Kirk drove up in his red jeep. He'd never come to the house before, and I was both scared and excited as he walked up to where I was sitting.

He flopped down on a flowered chaise, leaned his head back and closed his eyes. His hair drifted over one eyebrow, its clean blondness shimmering in the afternoon light. He was wearing tan shorts and a blue T-shirt, and as usual, I was struck by the beauty of his body. He was lean but muscular, yet not in an overbearing way.

Neither of us said anything for a while. Millions of things went through my mind but I didn't know how to begin or if I should. After all, *he'd* come to see *me*. I waited. Finally he opened his eyes.

I smiled.

He didn't.

It frightened me. I screwed up my courage and asked him why he'd come.

"That's a funny question."

"Is it? You've come to see me but you don't seem very friendly. I can't even get a smile out of you."

"I guess I feel too awful to smile," he said. "Oh, Anna, why didn't you tell me about Tony?"

Tony! How did he know about him? Then I remembered the first night with Nicki I'd told her all about him. She must have said something to Kirk. But I thought it didn't seem fair of him to mention this to me when he had Charlotte. Then he said:

"I can't stand deceit, dishonesty."

I looked at him quizzically.

"Yes, I know." He drew his legs up and sat cross-legged. "I feel like a rat deceiving Charlotte, but I explained that to you. I just didn't want to hurt her."

"Isn't that what men always say?" I asked in a worldly fashion.

"I don't know what men always say. How do *you* know?"

"I read a lot."

"We're getting off the subject. The subject being your boyfriend."

"I don't know why I didn't tell you, Kirk. I guess I just didn't see the point. I mean, you were with Charlotte and I didn't know what was happening with us, so why should I mention Tony? He didn't seem to have anything to do with anything. The truth is, Kirk, I thought you were just, I don't know, playing around with me. I guess that's why I didn't think I owed you anything, any explanations."

He leaned forward, his eyes searching my face as if he was looking for a lost treasure. "You thought I was playing around?"

"Why wouldn't I?"

He nodded. "Sure. You don't really know me."

I realized then that that was true. What *did* I know? I knew he was handsome and smart, and that he wanted to be a veterinarian. I *thought* he was gentle and sweet. Understanding. Kind. But was he? Those were the things I *wanted* him to be. But I didn't know him at all, not really.

Suddenly he said:

"Do you love Tony?"

76

I knew I didn't. Tony seemed like someone from another life to me now. Someone from my youth. Still, I was reluctant to tell Kirk the truth until I knew what he felt for me. I threw a question at him.

"Do you love Charlotte?"

He laughed. "Why are you turning things around?"

I should have known I couldn't get away with that.

"I just want to know," I said seriously.

"If I love Charlotte?"

"Yes."

"Oh, Anna, Anna. We shouldn't play games with each other. We'd better get things straight between us, okay? What about this turkey, Tony?"

That made me feel defensive. "He's not a turkey."

"He is to me."

This time when he smiled I felt it deep within me, as if he'd never smiled like that for anyone but me.

And then I heard myself saying: "I don't love Tony."

"I don't love Charlotte either," he said.

He got up and started toward me. My heart was making a terrible racket.

"Hi, there," Kate said.

Kirk whirled around and I jumped up. I could see that he was flushed and that his hands were in fists.

"Don't sneak up on a person like that," he snapped at Kate.

Kate's eyes immediately filled with tears. "I wasn't sneaking," she said, her lower lip trembling.

There was a strange moment when we all just stood there and I remember feeling frightened, but then Kirk said:

"Oh, hey, I'm sorry. You just scared me, that's all." He reached out for Kate but she backed up. I put my arm around her.

Kirk looked at me and shrugged. "I didn't mean to. . . . Well, I'll see you guys later."

And I did see him later. For the last time.

That was last night. And now it was the next day and Kirk was dead and Tony was up in the attic. I looked at my watch. It was eleven. I prayed Tony hadn't roasted up there. He must have been starving and lonely and maybe scared. I hoped he'd realize there was a good reason I hadn't come back for him.

Was I doing the right thing to hide Tony? I wondered. Why was he so afraid if he hadn't done anything? It was true that the islanders were suspicious of strangers, but everybody was a stranger to them unless you'd lived here a hundred years. And how did Tony know about that attitude? I recalled his use of Kirk's name and again it made me lose my breath. But what was I thinking? Tony hadn't murdered him. Then who had?

Larry? Nicky? Watson? Dick? Bill? Charlotte?

It was impossible to think of any of them as a murderer.

I crossed my arms over the windowsill, rested my chin on them and stared out at the blue water. Then I heard voices below and looked down. Detective Smolley and my parents had come out of the house.

They all shook hands and Smolley said:

"Thanks for your cooperation, Mr. Pahka."

"Glad to be of help."

They went to their respective cars and Smolley pulled

out first, Mom and Dad following. Next I saw Kate and Bill come out of the house and head toward the water.

Quickly I ran from my room and down the hall to the attic door. I pulled it open and hurried up the steep stairs. Even before I got to the top I could taste the musty smell and feel the oppressive heat. I hoped Tony hadn't passed out; I should have let him open a window.

I reached the top. There was the cot, the chair, the dresser. And that was all.

Tony was gone.

9

"What do you mean, Tony's been and gone?" Bill asked. Dick, Watson, Bill and I were sitting in a booth at The Cottage, a health food restaurant in Cranberry Harbor. Their specialty was blueberry muffins made with honey, and we each had one in front of us with something to drink.

I had never been anywhere with Dick or Watson without Kirk. It made me realize how little I knew either guy. Watson was the more difficult to know of the two. He was shyer and kind of awkward, much more Down East than Dick. You wouldn't say that Watson was funny-looking but you'd never call him handsome either. His brown hair was in a crew cut and he wore round, steel-framed glasses. He had full lips, a short nose and sometimes, if he didn't shave, straggly brown hair above his lip. And he was never out of his black-and-yellow waders. I couldn't understand how he could wear them all the time, even when it was very hot. I wondered if he wore them to bed!

Dick was much more polished than Watson, but then he'd had the advantage of a year away at college. Still, I guessed that Dick had always had some of that sophistication. And I was sure whatever smoothness he'd acquired had been learned from Kirk. But there was still a reticence about him, as if he wasn't totally comfortable in his own skin.

Because I was worried about what had happened to Tony, I had told them the story of his appearance and disappearance, leaving out one essential detail. I said he'd arrived at two in the morning and had thrown a pebble at my window, waking me. The rest of the story was the truth.

"So why did he take off?" asked Dick.

"I don't know."

"Well, now, let's just think a sec," Watson said slowly. "Maybe it just got too darn hot up there for him. Maybe he went somewheres to cool off while your folks was still around, don'tcha know." He absently rubbed a finger over the front of his crew cut.

"Then why didn't he come back when they left?" Dick asked. "No, I think there's more to it than that."

A ripple of fear coursed through me. Dick was very smart. Too smart.

"Like what?" Bill asked.

I held my breath.

Dick shrugged. "Who knows? But the whole thing sounds weird under the circumstances."

"Come on now, Dick," Watson said. "You don't even know this here Tony."

"And you do?" Dick asked sarcastically. His small brown eyes narrowed as he looked at Watson, irritated. "Listen, my best friend's been killed and I want to know who did it, okay?"

"We all want that."

"Do we?"

"Now just what's that supposed to mean?" Watson said, his full mouth going into a pout. He looked like a big baby.

"Forget it." Dick turned to me. "So maybe we should look for Tony. What do you want to do, Anna?"

What I wanted was to change the subject, get the attention off Tony, but I was afraid it would look queer after I'd brought it up. I was sorry I had, but his disappearance had made me feel uneasy and I hadn't counted on Dick's suspicious nature.

"I don't want to do anything. I think Tony will turn up," I said.

Bill said, "Tony's an okay guy, Dick. There's no reason to be suspicious of him. What would he want to kill Kirk for anyway?"

"Maybe you should ask your sister," Dick said.

"Me?" I squawked, feigning total innocence. How much did Dick know? I wondered. But why wouldn't he? He and Kirk were best friends. Hadn't I written Kristen about Kirk? Kirk must have told Dick everything.

"Well, now, let's wait a minute here. Do you know something, Anna? Something we should know?" Watson asked.

"Look, guys, Anna doesn't know anything more than the rest of us, so let's give her a break, okay?" Bill said protectively.

I pressed my knee against Bill's in thanks. "The only thing I know for sure is that Tony didn't kill Kirk."

"Are you sure Tony got to your house when he said he did?" Dick persisted.

"I looked at the time," I answered, pretending I didn't know what he was getting at.

"No, I mean maybe he got to the island earlier."

Watson said, "And what if he did? I mean, what if this dude did get to the island earlier, what's that got to do with the price of clams?"

Dick shrugged. "Figure it out."

"I don't think I like what you're implying, Dick," I said. My palms were starting to feel sweaty.

Dick slid down in his seat. "It was just a thought."

"A crummy one," I said.

"So who did it then?" Dick asked.

"Well, not Tony," I said.

"Not Tony and not Larry and not Charlotte and—"

"Oh, stop," I said.

"I guess we better face it, Anna," Watson said, fiddling with his glasses. "We just don't wanna think it's any of us, but it's gotta be somebody, don'tcha know."

A residue of orange clung to Bill's upper lip from his carrot juice. "Yeah, Watson's right."

"It still wasn't Tony," I said.

"Then why did he run away?" Dick asked.

I was getting ticked off. "He didn't run away." I popped the last piece of my muffin in my mouth. "He just left."

"Don't talk with your mouth full," Dick said.

"Who are you, my mother?"

"This is getting tacky," Bill said. "Let's not turn on each other, okay?"

You see, that's what I liked about Bill. He could be so grown up sometimes. I pinched him on the thigh to show him I thought he was neat, and he pinched me back.

We were all quiet for a minute, eating and drinking. Then Dick said:

"So what did you people think of Smolley?"

"A real jerk," Bill said.

"Yeah. I thought so, too. A hick," I said.

"Do you think he'll solve it?" Bill asked.

"He couldn't solve it if the murderer confessed," I said.

"Well, now, I wouldn't go underestimating Smolley," Watson said. He sucked on his straw and made a gross noise. "Sorry."

"You know him?" Bill asked.

"He's been around for a while." Watson had an irritating habit of not answering a question directly.

"So then you know him," I said.

"Old Smolley grew up here, then went off to Boston for a while. Came back here a few years ago."

He still hadn't answered the question but I let it go.

Dick said, "Smolley was some kind of big deal in Boston. He broke an important case there and got a lot of attention."

"That's right," Watson said. "Didn't like it, neither.

Came back here for peace and quiet, and look what happened."

"I don't know how good he was in Boston but I don't think he's very good now. I thought he asked a lot of dumb questions," I said.

Watson smiled, showing crooked teeth. "That's old Smolley for you. He likes to play dumb. It's an act, don'tcha know."

"I don't know if he was acting or not, but boy did he ever lean on me," Bill said.

"What do you mean?"

"Trying to get me to say I did it."

"You're kidding," I said.

"No way. He did. Didn't he do that to you?"

I shook my head. Bill looked at Watson and he shook his head.

"No," Dick said, "he didn't try that stuff with me, either."

The color seemed to drain from Bill's face and he swallowed hard, his Adam's apple bobbing in his neck.

"Nothing to worry about if there's nothing to worry about," Dick said, looking hard at Bill.

"I've got nothing to worry about," Bill said defensively. "I just didn't appreciate his technique, that's all."

"Sure," Watson said, "I wouldn't go for that neither. Makes you feel guilty even when you're not."

"That's right," Bill said almost cheerfully. "That's exactly right."

"Well," Dick said, "I think somebody ought to tell Smolley about your friend Tony."

"What for?" That was the last thing I wanted. Smolley would know then that I'd kept information from him and I'd look bad. Not to mention what Mom and Dad would say.

"Maybe this Tony knows something. Maybe he *saw* something. Did you ever think of that, Anna?"

"How could he see something when he wasn't even there?"

"Can you prove that? Can he?"

I jumped up. "You make me sick, Dick. Tony wasn't there. You just want to blame him because it's easier than blaming one of us."

Dick and I stared at each other for what seemed like an hour but was only a few seconds. Then he nodded and said, "I guess you're right. Forget it. I'm sorry, Anna." He held out his hand for me to shake. "Friends?"

I took his hand. "We're *all* upset," I said.

"When you lose someone like Kirk, well . . ." his sentence trailed off and he shook his head mournfully.

I glanced over at Watson and was shocked to see the look on his face. It was a cross between anger and scorn. I'd never seen him look like that. Watson was usually such a bland person that it was almost frightening to see his expression.

Then I saw him exchange a quick look with Bill, as if they were both in on something. All of it happened in seconds, and when it had passed I couldn't be sure it had taken place at all.

"Let's get out of here," I said.

We paid our check and started walking down the twisty street. Cranberry Harbor is very pretty. The streets are mostly cobblestone and the shops are in old buildings made of clapboard.

The main street ends at the water, and we turned in that direction when we reached it. We were just passing the bookstore when I saw him.

"I don't believe it. Look, Bill," I said.

Coming toward us was Peter Hallahan, Bill's nemesis.

"Oh, give me a break," Bill said.

"Well, well, well," Peter said as we converged on the sidewalk, "if it isn't the thief and his *tall* sister."

"What are you doing here?" Bill asked.

"Vacationing. What are you doing here? Or should I say, what are you stealing here?"

"Come on," Watson said, "I don't think this here guy's a friend."

"Brilliant," Peter said. "Who's this meat loaf, Sherlock Holmes?"

"Beat it, kid," Dick said.

Peter ignored him. "I hear you moved. Lucky for us in Maplewood, unlucky for your new friends here."

"Let's go," Watson said. He pulled at the sleeve of my shirt and we started down the street.

"I wonder if the good people of Blue Haven Island know they've inherited a criminal," Peter shouted after us as we walked away. "Don't let me catch you out alone at night, Parker. I'll be here for another week, so watch it."

We kept walking away from him, not looking back, and he kept yelling things. Once again I felt anger at Bill for having stolen the money.

Down at the bottom of the main street was a dock

with benches. We sat down and looked out at the boats. There was a great big white one that took tourists around the island, and it was loading while we watched.

Finally Bill broke our silence. "I guess I should tell you guys what that was all about."

"Well, now, Bill, you don't have to," Watson said in his leisurely way. "None of our business."

I looked over at Dick and could see that he wanted to know but was too polite to ask or pursue Bill's offer. Still, I thought it would be better to tell them. They could think that it was much worse than it was from what Peter had said.

"I think you should explain," I urged Bill.

He nodded, but I could see that he was really embarrassed. I wished then that I could help him, maybe tell the story myself, but I knew it was his responsibility. He cleared his throat and began.

When he was finished Watson ran a hand over his crew cut as if he was testing it for evenness and said, "I always say, what's past is past. Besides, sounds like you learned a whole lot about yourself from that shrink, Bill."

"I did." His face was covered with a thin film of sweat. "And the thing is I never in my life stole anything before. Or since."

"Got no doubts about it. And you got a lot of guts telling us like that. I admire you." He gave a friendly punch to Bill's shoulder.

Dick hesitated for a second, then agreed. "Me too. Anyway, stealing and murder are two very different things."

88

All of us looked at him, his words resounding in our ears like popping firecrackers. I don't think it had occurred to anyone else that Bill's theft might put him in a bad light in terms of the murder.

Dick could see that we were all surprised at his remark.

"I just meant that one thing has nothing to do with the other. I say we forget all about it, okay?"

We all agreed, but I knew no one was going to forget it.

Then Dick said, "I've been thinking. All we have to do is establish who was where when Kirk was killed, and then maybe we'll know who did it."

"Are you going to try and solve this, Dick?" I asked.

"I just want to help," he said meekly.

Bill said, "I didn't see anyone come near me."

"Me neither," said Watson.

"How about you?" Dick asked me.

"Here's the thing," I said. "I was the murderer. I killed Kirk. In the game, that is. And then I left him . . . alive."

"You're kidding," Bill said.

"Nope."

"Well, now, that means that some sucker went and killed Kirk with his own knife while we were all making tracks to home base. Whew! Somebody's crazy, don'tcha know," said Watson.

"Or really had it in for Kirk," Bill said.

"But who would?" I asked. "Everyone loved him."

The three guys just looked at me and said nothing.

"Well, didn't they?" I asked.

"Sure thing. Folks just loved Kirk Cunningham," Watson said sarcastically. "Nicest guy in town."

"Shut your mouth, Watson," Dick said, getting to his feet.

Watson put up his hands as if he was surrendering. "Back off now, just back off," he said.

"You back off."

"Right," Watson said.

The two of them glared at each other for a moment and then Dick stormed away.

"What was that about?" I asked Watson.

"Nothing," he said. "Just forget it."

"We'd better head back," Bill said.

As we walked to our car I thought over what had happened and knew I couldn't forget it. Something was very weird between Watson and Dick, and it had to do with Kirk. I realized then that maybe I was in the dark about Kirk. Maybe there were things about him that I didn't know. And just maybe they were things that weren't too nice.

10

The funeral was held in a small church in the town of Sealville on the island. All the houses (twelve of them) on the main road were painted white with red trim. A town ordinance decreed it. The church was at the end of the road and it was totally white.

Kirk had lived on Blue Haven Island all his life, so the church was packed. All of us connected to the restaurant, except Nicki and Larry, sat in the back on the right. I was sandwiched between Bill and Watson.

Smolley was there with two other men. I felt they were watching everyone, every expression, every move. It would have been bad enough without them, but they just made it worse.

The minister said that Kirk had been cut down before his time, and that he was a wonderful young man filled with life but now he'd gone on to a better place. I wondered. How did he know it was a better place? I guess that's what they mean by faith. But it's hard to have faith when terrible things happen. Why would God let Kirk be murdered?

The minister said that God moves in mysterious ways. I wondered again.

The Cunninghams sat in the front near the casket. All during the service you could hear Mrs. Cunningham sobbing. Mr. Cunningham was in a wheelchair in the aisle. He looked terrible. All his hair was gone, and there was a black spot on the back of his head where the radiation had been done. It seemed doubly cruel for him to have to go through this when he had so little time left.

I leaned forward a little to see Nicki. I could see her profile, and I was surprised to discover that she was dry-eyed. I shifted my gaze to Larry, but he was sitting in such a way that I couldn't see his face. From the stillness of his body I felt that he wasn't crying either. Only April was crying.

I was having a lot of trouble controlling my own tears. Not that I thought it was bad to cry or anything, but I felt as if I might go over the line into terrible sobs, and I didn't want to do that. I felt I didn't have the right, especially since most of the Cunninghams were controlling themselves. At any rate I held a handkerchief up to my eyes and swallowed the urge to cry out loud. I felt Bill take my hand. I turned to him and saw that he was looking at me very sympathetically. He squeezed my hand gently and I squeezed back.

Mom and Dad both had tears in their eyes and so did

Kate. But Watson and Dick were stone faced. And so was Charlotte. That really shocked me. Maybe it had something to do with the Yankee tradition. New Englanders are well known for their stoicism, so that must have been it. Still, I found it odd that Kirk's sister and girlfriend were so in control. Boys and men are intent on being what they think is strong, so it didn't surprise me too much that none of them were crying even though I thought it was dumb that they couldn't cry. But girls and women are expected to cry and in that we're very lucky. The whole thing is a big sexist mess, but nevertheless that's the way it is.

When the service was over the minister said that Mrs. Cunningham would lead the procession out. At the back of the church she would pull the red cord and ring the bell for Kirk. Then we were to follow and pull the cord, too. It was incredible. The bell didn't stop for a full ten minutes. Outside we all went to our cars. Bill and I rode together in the beat-up Ford I'd bought when we'd arrived on Blue Haven. We formed a procession and followed the hearse to the cemetery.

The minister said a prayer at the graveside and then we each took a small handful of dirt and threw it on the coffin. And that was it. It was over. Over for Kirk. Forever.

Now it was time to say something to Kirk's family. This was the hardest part.

"We have to say something to them," I told Bill.

"Yeah, I know. I feel like a jerk. I mean, I don't know what to say, do you?"

I shook my head. "I guess we can just say we're sorry."

"It seems so, I don't know, so . . . so . . ."

"Inadequate," I provided.

"Right."

"It is, but that's all there is to say."

"I guess."

Slowly we walked over to where the Cunninghams were standing. Mr. Cunningham had not come to the cemetery. A nurse had taken him back home. The rest of the family was standing in a line behind the casket, their backs to it. People were going up to them, kissing them, shaking their hands and mumbling appropriate words of condolence. Bill and I got at the end of the line.

A few minutes passed and then I found myself standing in front of Mrs. Cunningham. Her face was streaked with tears, and deep bluish circles were under her eyes. I couldn't help myself. I just burst into tears when I saw her face. And then I felt her hugging me. It was terrible. She was consoling me when it should have been the other way around. But it felt good to be in her arms, safe.

"It was God's will," I heard her whisper, and then I was sort of moved away and I stood in front of Nicki. I felt awful. I hadn't said a thing to Mrs. Cunningham. I looked back at her and saw that she was hugging Bill now.

"Hello, Anna," Nicki said flatly.

I turned back to her, my tears flowing freely. "Oh, Nicki," I said, "I'm so sorry."

"Thank you," she said tonelessly.

I looked into her eyes. They seemed to hold no emotion at all. I decided she was in shock. Then I moved on to Larry. He looked as numb as Nicki, and when I told him I was sorry he thanked me in the same flat way as she had. At least April showed some emotion.

At the car I asked Bill what he thought of the Cunninghams' behavior.

"I don't know, Anna. Maybe I'd act the same if you died. I guess it's one of those things you can't judge until it happens to you."

"Maybe so," I said.

I was thinking about that when Smolley came over to us.

"Maw-nin'," he said, and touched the brim of his white straw hat. He spoke in his exasperatingly slow way. "I wonder, Bill, if you would come on down to the station with me?"

"What for?" Bill asked.

"I reckon we'd just like some help with our investigation."

I stepped forward. "Do you want me to come too?"

"Nope. Thank you anyway, Anna. I reckon Bill will do just fine for now."

"What's up?" It was Dad. I felt relieved. He wouldn't let Smolley take Bill down to the station.

"Maw-nin', Mr. Pahka, Mrs. Pahka." He touched his hat again. "I was just askin' Bill here if he wouldn't mind helpin' us out."

"Helping you out how?" Dad asked.

"We'd like him to come down to the station for a bit, Mr. Pahka."

"What for?" Mom asked, lines creasing her forehead.

"We need some help with our investigation, ma'am."

"Oh, God," Mom said, "Jack."

Since Mom is a writer of mystery stories, she knew what that meant. I knew too, because I read them. They always say that when they suspect you.

"I thought you questioned him thoroughly yesterday," Dad said, putting a hand on Mom's arm.

"Yessir, I did, but I have a few more little questions Bill might be able to help me with. Leastways I think he can."

"Why can't you question him at our house?" Mom asked.

"Like to, but I can't. Now I'm not forcin' the boy to come, you understand, Mrs. Pahka. I'm just askin'." Smolley cocked his head to one side and stuck an unlit cigarette in his mouth.

"You have nothing to hide, Bill. I think you'd better go," Mom advised.

"But we'll come, too," Dad said.

"How about me?" I asked.

"No, Anna, you take care of Kate, okay?"

I agreed.

"Thank you kindly," Smolley said. "It won't take but a bit. Come along, son."

"Can't he ride with us?" Dad asked indignantly.

"It's all right, Jack," Mom said.

"Better if he comes with me," said Smolley.

I gave Bill's arm a pat and he smiled back at me, faint as it was. It's funny being a twin, different from just being brother and sister, or sister and sister. I love Kate and lots of times I think I know how she's feeling. But with Bill I *know* how he's feeling. Sometimes we're like the same person. Often when we've been apart we've known what the other one was thinking and feeling. It's weird.

I knew now that Bill was scared. It wasn't just that I could see it on his face—I could feel it in my stomach, hear it in my mind. I wished I could go with him, give him support.

"Will you kids be okay?" Dad asked.

"Sure," I said, "don't worry." I gave Dad a kiss, reassuring him.

We watched them go. Watson and Dick came up to us as we went to my car.

"What's going on?" Dick asked.

I filled them in.

"Well, now, that seems real poor."

"It's probably nothing," Dick said. "I bet they take each one of us in during the next couple of days. Smolley's got nothing better to do and he has to look busy."

"Will Bill be okay?" Kate asked, tears in her eyes.

"Oh, sure, honey," I said. I put my arm around her and held her to me. "Don't worry, Kate. Really. Listen to Dick."

When I said that, I saw a strange look pass over Watson's face. It disappeared as quickly as it had come. Then I remembered their argument the day before at the wharf. There was no love lost between those two.

"Nothing to worry about, Kate," Dick was saying, "nothing at all. This is just part of an investigation. Cheer up."

"Okay," she said unconvincingly.

"Tell you what," Dick went on, "I think we should go

down to Jordon's Wharf and have a soda or something, okay?"

He gave Kate a hug around her shoulders and she gave him a weak smile. I was grateful to him, because I didn't have it in me to cheer up Kate.

We piled into my car and headed out of Sealville. I drove past Sandy Beach. It's called that, but the beach isn't really made of sand. From a distance, up on the road, it gives the appearance of a sandy beach, but what it's really made of is millions and millions of broken shells. When the sun hits it, the white of the shells sometimes hurts your eyes, but mostly it's beautiful.

I turned toward Bass Point. Blue Haven Island is like two fists connected at the wrists with water between them. At the bottom of the right fist a knuckle sticks out, and that's Bass Point. Sometimes we liked to go down there to sit on Jordon's Wharf. It was another lobster restaurant—or lobster pound, as it was called—but of course we never ate any of that stuff, having so much of it. What we did was to stop at a little dessert stand nearby, pick up a strawberry tart or a slice of heavenly peach pie and then go over to the Wharf and sit at one of the picnic tables overlooking the water, drinking soda and eating our goodies.

We did that today. They were out of our favorites, so Kate and I each got blueberry buckle and the guys got slices of apple pie. Dick bought us each a soda. On the Wharf we sat at the first table by the water, Kate and I with our backs to it.

No one said anything for a while. We all seemed to be concentrating on our food. I took a bite of my buckle and looked at both of the guys, who were working on their pies. It was weird seeing them in suits and ties. I never had before. Dick seemed comfortable in his, but Watson appeared awkward. Maybe it was because his suit jacket was slightly small, the sleeves too short and the shoulders too narrow. But aside from that I guessed I was so used to seeing him in his T-shirts, jeans and yellow-and-black waders that I had a hard time reconciling this Watson with the one I saw every day.

It had been a cloudy morning, but now the sun was breaking through and I thought the guys must have been hot. I knew I wished I was in a T-shirt and shorts instead of this dumb dress I'd had to wear.

"Why don't you guys take off those jackets and ties?" I said.

They both looked at me gratefully and immediately undid ties and shed their jackets.

"Whew," Watson said. "Now that's better. Can't remember the last time I wore a suit. Must've been my grandpa's funeral."

Dick looked at him, slightly disgusted. "I like wearing a suit on occasion. Not on occasions like this, of course. Don't you like wearing dresses, Anna?"

"Sometimes. When I have a date."

Dick nodded in agreement and smiled at me like we were on the same side or something. I didn't have any desire to get into the battle he and Watson had going, so I smiled quickly and looked away. The silence that followed was filled with tension until I broke it.

"I guess Larry and Nicki are really wiped out, huh?"

Watson took off his glasses and cleaned them with his

tie. He was very tan from being out on the water, and he looked like he was squinting in the sun all the time.

"Well, now," he said, "your brother dying is bad enough, but him getting murdered is a whole different can of worms, don'tcha know." He put his glasses on over the bridge of his long pointy nose, gave a nod as if to punctuate his statement and went back to his apple pie.

"I can't think of anything worse," I said.

"Do we have to talk about it?" Kate said, looking very pale.

"Of course we don't," Dick said.

I felt very annoyed at both Kate and Dick. They started talking about some television show and I tuned out. I found myself in a stare, looking past the guys up toward the parking lot, and then I almost fell off the bench. There was Tony! He was getting out of a truck and carrying a basket of lobsters. I watched him take the basket inside the restaurant. Kate hadn't seen him, and the others had their backs to him.

I excused myself and went up the boardwalk toward the restaurant. I waited near the door, and in a moment he came out.

"Anna! Boy, are you a sight for sore eyes," he said, as if I was the one who'd disappeared.

"Me? Tony, where have you been?"

"It's a long story, and right now I've gotta get goin'. I'm working for this guy, Wilbur Jessup. Got a room over his garage, too. I was plannin' to come by tonight, okay?"

"How could you have just run out that way? Didn't you think I'd worry?" I asked.

100

"You knew I'd be okay," he said, genuinely surprised by the idea I might be upset.

"Hey, Tony, let's go," a boy called from the truck.

"Gotta go, Anna. Listen, you didn't tell anybody, did you? I mean about when I got here. I'm sayin' I got here yesterday afternoon, about one. Okay?"

I nodded, not really answering his question.

"I'll come by tonight. Maybe you could soften your parents up before I get there. You could say you saw me right here. Yeah, that's a good idea. Gotta go, honey." He leaned down and kissed me lightly on my lips.

He ran to the truck, jumped in. The truck backed up and Tony waved as they pulled out.

I couldn't believe it. What an operator. Here two days and already he had a job and a room. Slowly I walked back to the table. Everybody was looking my way, so I knew they'd all seen Tony. Dick's lower lip was sort of jutting out and he had a frown on his usually peaceful face.

"Who was that?" he asked.

I didn't know what to say. But Kate took care of that.

"That's Tony, Anna's boyfriend. What's he doing here?"

I didn't answer her.

"So that there's him, huh?" Watson said.

"That's him," I said.

"Thought you said he didn't get on the island 'til late at night. Two, you said."

"That's right." I suddenly felt scared. "Why?"

"Well, now," Watson said. "That there guy you were talking to didn't get here at any two o'clock."

I had a terrible sinking feeling.

"What do you mean, Watson?" Dick asked.

"Mean I saw him hitchhiking earlier. When I was driving over to the restaurant, night of the murder, I saw that dude on the road. It was about nine, I guess. Didn't pick him up 'cause I didn't like the looks of him."

I felt myself blushing.

Dick said, "So what's the story, Anna?"

"I don't know," I said. "All I know is that he threw a pebble at my window at two in the morning."

"You sure?" Watson asked.

I hated lying. And I especially hated lying for Tony when I didn't know what the truth really was. It was still impossible for me to believe he could have killed Kirk, but that's the way I felt about everyone. Even so I went on lying.

"I'm sure," I said.

"Why is it I don't believe you, Anna?" Dick said.

"I'm leaving," I said, starting to get up.

Dick put his hand on my shoulder and kept me sitting.

"I hate this," Kate said, putting her head down on the table.

"Me too," I said.

"Better tell us," said Watson. "If this dude Tony's innocent there's nothing to worry on."

Dick looked at me, his eyes riveting mine. "Anna, this is serious. Was Tony at the restaurant the night Kirk was killed?"

I felt terrible. If I said yes I'd be betraying Tony, but if I said no, not only would I be lying, I might be shielding a murderer. But Tony was innocent, and in that case nothing bad could happen to him.

"Anna," Dick demanded, "tell us the truth."

And so I did.

11

Two hours after the revelation at Jordon's Wharf I was sitting in a sea-polished curve inside a cliff of salmon-colored granite rock. It was about a half mile from our house. In fact I could see the cliff from my window. I'd discovered the indentation almost as soon as I'd arrived on Blue Haven and had decided immediately that it was a good place to think. Across from me on the lowlands cormorants made their nests.

Early in the morning the birds would leave their nests, usually two by two, and fly to their fishing grounds. They had long necks and their wings moved faster than the gulls'. I liked the feeling of serenity they gave me.

But now they were nowhere in sight and I felt far from serene. There was so much to think about, to figure out. Dick and Watson were convinced that Tony had killed Kirk. They said if he hadn't he wouldn't have asked me to lie about his arrival time. Yet he'd stayed on the island. Why? They said it was because he wanted to be near me. The whole thing just confused me, and I felt as if I was going round and round.

The worst part was that Watson and Dick had said it was my duty to tell Smolley about Tony. I argued with them, then finally promised I would tell my parents when they came home and see what they decided. But now as I sat here looking out at the water, the sun reflecting and giving it an appearance of quicksilver, I wondered if I would.

First of all, Mom and Dad would be furious with me for not having told them before. And secondly, I didn't want to betray Tony. At least I should wait until I saw him again, I thought.

My mind shifted to thoughts of the funeral, and then I remembered my short conversation with Watson when I'd let him off at his house. I'd already dropped Dick back at the church, where he'd left his car. Watson was stepping out when I put a hand on his arm. He stopped and looked at me. I glanced at Kate, who was in the back seat, and fortunately she seemed to be in a world of her own. Softly I said:

"Could I ask you something?"

"Sure thing."

"Did Charlotte really love Kirk?"

A flush began at the base of his scrawny neck and quickly worked its way up into his face like mercury in a hot thermometer. Matters of love, I thought, were not something he was used to speaking about.

"Dunno, Anna. Guess you'll have to ask her."

"She didn't shed one tear at the funeral," I said.

"Aw, that's just the way Yankees are, I reckon."

Suddenly he was sounding more Down East than ever. I thought it must be out of nervousness. He didn't like my questions. Still, I had to know. I had the distinct feeling that there was something going on, some strangeness that other people knew about and I didn't.

"Watson, I think you know something I don't know. Is it something about Kirk?"

"Don't know what you mean, Anna." He looked away, down at his feet.

I took a deep breath and dove into the next question. "Did you like Kirk?"

I watched his mouth twitch and then he quickly got out of the car. He shut the door and poked his head back in, his glasses askew.

"Don't know why you're asking all these here questions, but my advice is stay out of this. Kirk was sorta hard to understand and . . . well, you hardly knew him."

"I knew him better than you think," I said foolishly.

"Did you?"

I didn't know whether to confide in him or not. Besides, Kate was in the back and I felt funny talking about this stuff in front of her.

"Can we have a talk some other time?" I asked.

"Nothing to talk about, Anna. Trust me. Forget Kirk. Forget everything." He pulled his head out of the window and hurried away toward his house.

Thinking about that conversation now, I couldn't make any more sense out of it than I had at the time. But I was more convinced than ever that there was something mysterious that I didn't know about. Watson wanted me to drop my questioning, Why? Had he killed Kirk? Did he know who had?

This was pointless. I could ask myself a million questions, but none of it would do any good unless I got more concrete information. But who would talk to me? Who would answer my questions? Dick was Kirk's best friend, and Nicki and Larry were unapproachable at this point. Charlotte? Never. Maybe I should talk to Mom.

Maybe when they got back with Bill from seeing Smolley, I should ask her for some ideas. Surely she had some. It must have been weird for her to always be writing about murder and then be smack in the middle of one in real life. I wondered if she'd put on her Libby Crawford hat and try and solve it. But maybe because it was real it was different for her. I'd have to ask.

I thought of Kirk. I missed him. My eyes clouded over. The sea and sky became blurred. I reached for a tissue and found my notebook and pen instead. I took them out of my pocket. Maybe if I wrote a poem I'd feel better. I wasn't a very good poet, but often if I wrote about things it helped.

I sat for quite a while and then something came to me. I wrote several versions and finally I liked what I had. I read it over:

Visions of you haunt me,
love.
Inside I weep,
and my heart aches as
silence creeps.
Over me, you fly so free.
God's forever taken you
from me.

As I was reading it a second time, I heard a noise and I froze. There was a crunching sound, footsteps on the rocks, and they were coming toward me, closer and closer. And then he was there, looming over me.

"Hi, Anna," Tony said.

"Tony," I yelled, "you've got to stop doing this. You're always frightening me." I felt like crying, I was so scared. "How did you find me anyway?"

"Some swell greeting," he said.

"I'm sorry, but you scared me half to death."

He plunked himself down next to me and reached out to touch my hair. Instinctively, I pulled back. His eyes darkened.

"Thanks, friend," he said sourly.

He looked so pitiful I found myself feeling very badly for him. "Oh, Tony," I said.

"Aren't you at all glad to see me?"

"Well, sure I am, but you scared me, that's all."

"Sorry about that. Kate told me where you were. I don't know how else I could have come here. I mean, I wasn't tiptoein' or anything."

"Yeah, I guess you're right. But I thought you were coming over tonight."

"I finished my work early. Listen. I left the attic because I was suffocatin' up there, and I figured I wouldn't be able to get out for hours. Anyway, I thought it might be hard on you to have me up there."

"You were right," I said. "Everybody hung around forever."

He nodded as if to say that he'd done the right thing. "Anyway, we can have the summer we planned, because I'm goin' to be able to stay until I have to go into the Air Force. Isn't that neat?"

"Neat," I said, trying to sound enthusiastic.

"What's this?" he asked, pulling my notebook out of my hand.

"Tony, don't," I cried.

But he had it and was reading the poem. I watched as the familiar dark look came over his face. Dr. Doom was here with me in my secret hiding place. Slowly he turned to look at me.

"You write that?" he asked.

I nodded.

"I don't get it," he said.

"What do you mean?"

"Well, what's this line mean, 'God's forever taken you from me'?"

I didn't know what to answer so I said nothing.

He went on. "This thing's not about me, is it?"

I was terrified of admitting the truth, but I couldn't not answer and there was no point in pretending the poem was about him. Finally, I said, "No, it's not about you."

He pressed his lips together and the muscle in his cheek kept jumping. "It's about that guy who was killed, huh?"

"Yes," I whispered.

He grabbed my arm and squeezed hard. "What was goin' on between you two, anyway?"

"Tony," I said, "you're hurting me."

"Answer me," he insisted, still squeezing.

"Nothing was going on. Let go," I yelled

He did.

"Sorry. Sometimes I don't know my own strength. So talk, okay?"

"Look, Tony, you don't own me," I said.

"I thought you were my girl."

"I was."

"Was?"

He looked so sad, so hurt, I didn't know what I felt. Except that I was a bit afraid of being up here with him alone. There were no houses nearby, no people. The pulse in my neck began to throb.

"Listen," I said, "do you want to walk down to the beach?"

"No. I want to talk about this, Anna. About us."

"Sure. I just thought . . ." I let my sentence trail off because I really didn't know what to say. I told myself I was being dumb. There was no reason to be afraid of Tony. Was there?

"What's going on, Anna? Where do we stand?"

I relaxed a little going back to the conversation. If he

110

was willing to talk, he wasn't about to do anything. But do what? I had to stop thinking that way.

"What do you mean, where do we stand?" I asked.

"Did you love that guy?"

"I don't know," I said honestly.

He started to laugh. Normally at first and then it changed and he sounded maniacal.

"Stop it, Tony," I said.

He kept on laughing and tears formed in the corners of his eyes and ran down his cheeks. I wanted to get away from him, but I was sure he'd stop me if I tried to run. Again I told him to stop laughing, but he went right on. The sound chilled me, the hair on my arms standing straight up. At last the laughter tapered off and he wiped the tears from his face. And then he spoke.

"You think I didn't know? Huh? You think this is some big surprise?"

I shrugged, not knowing what to say.

"I saw you that night," he said. "I saw you kiss that creep. I saw the whole thing." Tony's fists were clenched in front of him and he was shaking.

Suddenly I was sure he'd killed Kirk, and just as sure that he was going to kill me. I had to try and save myself.

"Tony, listen. It didn't mean anything. I don't care what you saw, it wasn't important. I was just flirting, that's all. You have to believe me."

"Yeah? Well, what about this poem?"

"It's nothing. Honest."

"I don't believe you, Anna."

"Well, it's true. It's you I love, Tony. Really."

"How come you didn't know that a minute ago?"

"You had me confused, that's all. Believe me, Tony. I love you."

"You sure?"

"I'm sure."

He moved closer to me, his hands touching my shoulders. My muscles tensed. I felt his strong fingers kneading my shoulders. It almost hurt. I wanted to push his hands away but I couldn't. I kept staring straight ahead, afraid to look at him. His breath was on my cheek, near my ear.

"My parents will be home soon," I whispered. "I have to get back."

He said nothing.

"And Kate," I said.

He kissed my neck, his lips warm on my skin.

"What about Kate?" he asked, his words almost muffled by my throat.

"She'll be coming up to get me soon," I lied.

"Not with me here," he said.

I felt his right hand slip from my shoulder up to my face, a finger traced the outline of my chin and then the hand dropped to my throat, fingers reaching, reaching. I thought my heart would stop with fear, and finally I found the strength to push him away.

"Hey, what's that for, huh?"

"I thought I heard someone," I said, hoping he'd believe me.

"I didn't hear anything." He listened and then turned back to me. "There's no one around, Anna. We're all alone."

I felt as if I might pass out from fear. Tony Nardone

112

was a stranger, a stranger who might be a killer. And if he had killed once, he wouldn't be afraid to kill again. He reached out and pulled me to him, crushing my lips to his. His hands moved from my back up, up toward my head while his fingers reached in under my hair, then slowly slid down my neck. Finally I felt his thumbs on my throat. There were seconds when it was as if I was paralyzed, but then I found my strength and began to struggle. His hands gripped me tighter and I felt the pressure of his thumbs. Then, just as suddenly as he had begun, he pulled away.

It was then that I heard Kate calling me.

"I love you," he whispered.

I touched my throat. It didn't really hurt. Had I imagined it?

"It's Kate," I whispered, grateful for her unexpected call.

"Yeah, I heard."

We both stood up, and I stepped out onto the ledge of my minicave. I saw Kate some yards away and called out to her.

"Mom and Dad are back and they want you to come home," she shouted.

"I'll be right there," I said. "Tony, I have to go."

"Okay. Can I come over tonight?"

"No. I don't think you'd better. I need some time to talk to them and stuff, okay?"

He looked disappointed. "Okay, but you tell them I'm here, understand?"

I didn't like his tone—it frightened me; but I told him I would. "Come to the restaurant tomorrow night."

I would be safe there with everyone around. I was not planning to be with Tony alone again. "I have to go now. Wait about ten minutes, and then you can go too."

He reached out for me but I evaded him. " 'Bye," I called, not looking back to see how he had taken that.

When I got to the house I had pulled myself together somewhat, but the minute I saw Mom and Dad I knew something was very wrong. "Where's Bill?" I asked.

Neither answered. Then Dad asked me to sit down. I did.

"What is it?" My head was spinning and my heart careened off the wall of my chest.

Dad said, "We mustn't be despairing. God knows it's a mistake."

"What?" I said, almost crying.

"Bill's been arrested."

"Arrested? Why?"

Mom knelt down in front of me and took my hands in hers. "Don't worry, Anna, it'll all work out. But for now Bill's been charged with Kirk's murder."

"But why? Why Bill?"

Mom and Dad exchanged a look, and then Mom said so softly I almost didn't hear:

"His fingerprints were on the knife."

12

Bill's arrest solved one problem. If he was the murderer then Tony wasn't. That is if you believed Bill was guilty. I didn't.

You don't spend seventeen years with a person and not know him a little bit. And I knew my twin brother more than a little bit.

It was true that in the last year or so we'd drifted apart, but even so, inside we'd never really separated. I felt I knew Bill like I knew myself. Oh, sure there are things about myself I don't know. Things I hide from. Everybody does that to some degree. There are traits I have that I'm sure I deny and attitudes that elude me altogether. But the basic stuff I know about. Like good and bad. I know that intrinsically I'm a good person even though I might make mistakes here and there.

And I know that about Bill, too.

Okay, so he stole over three hundred dollars that he'd been entrusted with. That's pretty bad, I'll admit. But stealing and killing are two different things, like Dick said. Your average thief doesn't kill unless he's caught in the act, trapped, so to speak. And the murder of Kirk Cunningham had nothing to do with theft. So even if Bill was your average thief, it still wouldn't hold up.

But my brother is *not* your average thief. He stole *once*. And he did it because he needed help. I'm not saying I condone his theft, but there was a logic to it. It had nothing to do with being bad. Nothing to do with evil. Nothing to do with being insane. Murder is done by either an evil person or an insane one. My twin is neither. I'd stake my life on it.

There is definite good in William S. Parker. Sweetness, too. He's a gentle guy who has been known to give his lunch to some of the poorer kids in school. I've seen him do it. Something I've never had the compassion to do. Few have. And all through his sophomore year he went once a week to the Briarcliff Nursing Home to read to the old people. Once I went with him and found it too depressing, couldn't bear the smells. But Bill never complained.

I've never heard him say anything really rotten about anyone or make fun of the nerds in school the way the rest of us have. Even when his height wasn't an issue, he was always for the underdog.

But by his junior year I guess being only five feet four got to him. *He* was now the butt of the jokes, the guy the others put down. And the girls he liked were always taller than he. And even through we'd drifted apart in the year that preceded the theft, I knew he was going through a painful time. But I couldn't reach him. Oh, who was I kidding? I didn't even try. I'd been hurt by his withdrawal, taken it personally, made myself the center of the universe. So the result was that I refused to see that it was my brother who needed something from me instead of the other way around.

By the time his theft came to light, I was so involved in my own hurt feelings, I didn't even try to understand why he'd done it. And then it was all exacerbated by his being instrumental in our lives' changing so drastically. I got mad and stayed mad. I'd barely had a conversation with him since January, so I didn't have the slightest idea what was going on with him. Except I knew one thing.

He hadn't killed Kirk.

I didn't care if the knife had his *body print* on it, my brother was innocent. But at this point my knowing that wasn't going to do him much good. For instance, Smolley wasn't going to look any further. He would be satisfied with Bill's arrest. So unless somebody confessed, my brother was in one heck of a fix. And that meant that someone had to solve this thing. It was clear to me that Mom was too emotionally upset to do any detective work, so that left only one person. Me.

Okay, so I'll be the first to admit it—my credentials are a little shaky. But I've always loved puzzles, and my mind tends to work that way, deducing things, putting two and two together. Besides, my mom lets me read her books when she's halfway through to see if I can solve the mystery, and I often do. It makes her really mad and she screams and yells, but in the end she's grateful to me. The point is Mom is a very good writer, known for her ingenious plots, has won the Mystery Writers of America Award twice—and *I* often defeat her. It's simply that I'm very methodical, very logical. Plus, Mom says I'm pretty smart.

So that's what I have going for me. I guess it isn't much but it's all I've got. It'll have to do.

As for Tony, I told my parents the truth. I had to. For a number of reasons. One, I thought it might help Bill, and two, I was beginning to wonder about Tony myself. If Smolley checked him out and found him innocent, then I'd feel a lot better . . . a lot safer.

Mom and Dad were really understanding about my not having told them about Tony before. Had I known how they'd react, I would have told them from the beginning. Sometimes it's easy to forget how neat your parents can be.

Dad called Smolley early this morning and told him about Tony and where to find him, so we'll see what happens. I didn't mention anything about Tony's hands on my throat, or the fear I'd experienced, because I didn't think that was fair. I mean, maybe I just imagined the whole thing . . . making it ominous when it was really romantic. Anyway, I'm bound and determined to solve this case.

Today we were opening the restaurant for the first time since the murder. Mom said we had seventeen reservations so far. Dad asked me to come in early because he's shorthanded without Bill.

I reached the restaurant at eleven o'clock. Mom and

Dad, and Dick and Charlotte, were already there. At least their cars were. Charlotte was probably gathering seaweed and Dick driftwood. I went inside the cabin, where Mom was already washing steamers and Dad was making his pies. I kissed them both. They looked so sad, so worried. Bill would not be out on bail until tomorrow morning. I thought about telling them I was going to solve the whole thing, but I knew it would only make them worry more, so I kept my mouth shut. "Take a break, Mom," I said as I moved in next to her at the steamer vats.

"I need to be working," she said.

I understood. Picking up a small steamer, I began my day's work.

Cleaning the steamers is the worst job, and it was one that was shared. Cleaning steamers sucks. You have to put them in great vats of water with cornmeal and let them sit. Then you scrub them with a handbrush . . . each and every little one. It takes about a half hour for every pound, and some nights we used as much as sixty pounds. Mom, Nicki, Charlotte and I got stuck with this job most of the time. I think there was a little sexism going on, but no one said anything. Anyway, everyone had their assigned job.

Watson delivered the lobsters and steamers; Bill, Larry, Dick and, of course, Kirk, when he was alive, got driftwood and seaweed and tended the fires. Dad baked. Different people made coffee and drew the butter. We all took turns serving. There were no dishes to be washed, because no utensils were used and only paper plates were offered. Everything was eaten with your hands.

119

Before coming to Maine I'd always had broiled lobsters and eaten them with forks. But lobsters made this way are just pulled apart as you eat them. The first week I ate one every night and finally got sick as a dog. Now I have one about once a week.

Silently, Mom and I scrubbed side by side. I wanted to say a million things, to break the sadness, but my mouth felt stuck. Mom finally interrupted the quiet.

"I just can't believe that I spend my life writing about murder and now my own son has been arrested and there's not a thing I can do," she said.

I looked at her closely. She was really a very good-looking woman for someone middle-aged. But today her eyes looked puffy and I missed the wonderful smile she usually had on her face.

"Can't you think like Libby?" I asked.

"I can't even think like me," she said. "My mind feels like mush."

It was clearer than ever that I'd have to do this on my own. I couldn't even use her for a sounding board the way Libby sometimes used one character or another.

The door of the cabin opened and Charlotte came in.

"It's really hot today," she said.

Her blond hair was in two pigtails, tied with pink ribbon. She was wearing running shorts and a T-shirt that said CRANBERRY HARBOR. Our eyes met and I noted that her usual dislike of me was shining through.

"Have a soda, Charlotte," Dad said.

"Think I will."

I kept scrubbing my steamers and trying to look at Charlotte from the corner of my eye. She was no longer just Charlotte Coombs, seventeen, a native of Blue Haven Island. She was no longer a rival. She was no longer just a pain in the butt. She was a suspect.

Kirk was stabbed in the back. And the knife had plunged in to the hilt. I knew from my reading that that took a bit of strength, but plenty of women stab people.

Charlotte lifted a soda to her lips and I took in the size of her hand. It was medium but sturdy-looking, the fingers kind of short and squared off at the tips. Her arms were well developed and I had seen Charlotte lift a crate of lobsters fairly easily. She was definitely in the running. There was only one problem. Motive. Unless she knew about Kirk and me. But would she kill him for that? Of course she'd had a breakdown, so who knew what she might do under stress? I had to find out what she knew.

I pulled my hands out of the cornmealy water, dried them on my apron and said to my mother that I was taking a little break. She nodded, smiling faintly.

Charlotte had gone outside and was sitting on a bench at one of the tables. I had no desire to be near her, but now it was my job.

"Mind if I join you?" I asked.

She looked surprised. No wonder. I'd never voluntarily spent a moment with her before. She shrugged.

"Free country," she said unpleasantly.

I sat down across from her. She was sucking on a cigarette and smoke drifted from her nostrils. It was not a pretty sight. I tried to think how to start, and then I hit on the idea of simply imitating Libby Crawford. Libby was a woman up in years, but she was spry and active

121

and solved the most difficult cases. And it seemed to me she did it by asking questions and listening carefully.

Libby always leaped right in, so that's what I did.

"I guess you're missing Kirk terribly, aren't you?"

"Am I?" She stared past me, into the woods.

"You don't miss him?"

"I guess it seems strange that he's not here." She looked at me, her eyes like two blue chips of cobalt glass.

I was stunned. Surely it must have felt more than strange to her. But then I reminded myself of her delicate mental state. Still, it had been an odd way of putting it. I continued.

"But you were always together. You must feel a loss."

"I suppose," she murmured, looking at her fingernails. Obviously Charlotte had a tough time with feelings, I noted. This did not, of course, make her a killer. Most people have a tough time with feelings. What would Libby do now? I wondered. Press on.

"He was such a cheerful person, so happy all the time," I said.

"Who?"

This startled me. Who did she think I was talking about? "Kirk, of course."

"Oh, Kirk. Kirk." She looked at me, her expression going from a blank to something that looked really ugly. "Why are you asking me all these questions?" she snarled.

"I guess I—"

"I knew about the two of you, you know."

Her words hit me like a slap across the face. "Listen," I said, "there was—"

"Don't bother to deny it, Anna. Kirk told me all about it when it started."

Now I was sure she was lying. But if she'd found out, it was certainly a possible motive.

"I suppose he didn't tell you that he'd told me, huh? What did he say, that I'd had a nervous breakdown once and I was too fragile to tell?"

I was speechless. I guess my mouth fell open, because Charlotte started to laugh. It wasn't exactly a mean laugh. I guess it was more pitying than anything.

She shook her head back and forth, back and forth. "You poor dope. Well, you weren't the first."

"But, but . . . why?" I finally got out.

"Why what?"

"If that's true, why did you stay with him?"

"Because I . . . Oh, never mind. You wouldn't understand." She jumped up from the bench and strode away, back toward the beach.

I could have easily caught up with her, but I was too wiped out by what she'd said. There was no proof that Kirk had told her about us—she might have discovered that on her own—but how did she know Kirk had told me about her nervous breakdown? Had she really had one or not? And what did she mean that I wasn't the first?

It wasn't too hard to figure out. Charlotte was trying to have me believe that Kirk flirted with lots of girls and that he always told them he couldn't tell Charlotte because she'd had a breakdown. But how did I know if Charlotte was telling the truth? Maybe there was some truth mixed up with the lies. I felt sick. Being a detective could be dangerous.

Sometimes you found out things you didn't want to know!

13

Mom always wore a long dress and sandals when she was doing her hostess number. She'd go around to the various tables and chat with the customers, asking them where they were from and laughing at their stories. They all had stories. She made everyone feel good; people liked my mother. She was charming and gregarious and smart. And most of all, she enjoyed it. Usually. But this night she was having a rough time. Her son was in jail for murder.

I watched her as she went through her routine with the customers, and probably none of them knew she was suffering. But I did. I could see it in the way she held her shoulders, the way she walked, a little less spring in her step. Still, the show had to go on. And that's what it was like. Running a restaurant is like putting on a show every night. You never knew what might happen.

Dad wasn't himself either. Most nights he wandered around and chatted with customers, too. But tonight he stayed near the pit as if he had to watch the fire, which was Dick's job. His brown eyes had that droopy, sad look, and nothing I or anyone did changed it.

I was dishing out some steamers to a fat lady in a green polyester pants suit when Nicki joined me. I was surprised to see her. Neither she nor Larry had been expected.

"Thank you," Green Polyester said.

"You're welcome."

"Tell me," she said, a piece of gray hair trailing across her cheek like a scar, "are you all one big happy family?"

"No, we're two families." I didn't think I needed to tell her we weren't very happy right now.

She nodded as if my answer had made her evening and went to her table.

"Hi, Nicki," I said.

"Sorry I'm late," she answered.

"We didn't expect you at all."

"No? How come?"

This was getting weirder and weirder. I wanted to say, "Haven't you noticed, your brother's been murdered," but I didn't. Instead I said:

"Well, under the circumstances."

"That's over now," she said as if I was a fool for thinking otherwise.

Over? How could it be over? I wondered if she knew about Bill. I was going to ask her, but a man in a blue

126

T-shirt and red plaid pants stood in front of me waiting for his plate of steamers.

"Pile them up," he commanded. "Might as well, or I'll be back for seconds." He laughed, and it sounded like a donkey.

"That's all right," I said, "we like people to come back for seconds."

"Oh, let's just get it all done in one trip," he insisted.

Although the paper plates were of the heavy-duty variety, I knew how much could fit on them without spilling over. "I don't think any more will fit," I said, growing impatient.

"They'll fit in my tum-tum," he said, and laughed again.

Nicki and I just looked at him. I held out the plate and finally he walked away. The next customer was a short, thin woman who looked like she could use a double portion. I gave her a few extra.

There was a break before the next customer, and I took that opportunity to ask Nicki if she knew about Bill.

"I heard," she said.

"Do you believe it? I mean, do you believe Bill did it?" I was feeling very anxious, wondering what she thought.

She shrugged. "I don't know. I suppose he could have," she answered flatly.

"Don't you care?" I burst out.

Nicki looked at me blankly.

127

Just then a young couple with a baby came up to the serving line. The baby was in a carrier on the man's back and seemed to be asleep. Nicki and I each handed them their steamers.

"This is a neat place," the man said.

"Thanks," I said.

"We heard about Cunningham's Clambake all the way out in Washington State," the woman said.

We'd kept the original name because it had such a good reputation.

"It's our first night on the Island, and this is where we came," she said, smiling and showing two round dimples.

"I hope you enjoy it," I said, wanting to get back to my conversation with Nicki.

"Oh, we will." They went off to a table and I saw that the baby was just waking up. I hoped it wouldn't start howling.

There were four more people to wait on and then there was another lull. I turned back to Nicki.

"What I meant before," I said, "was don't you care that your brother was murdered and that my brother has been accused of murdering him?"

"I care very much," she said, her brown eyes growing misty.

I felt a sense of relief.

But then she said, "If Bill did it, well, I just don't know what I'll do."

I stared at her. What did that mean?

"Ready for my lobster and corn," a huge man in a white golf cap said.

128

Nicki lifted the tarpaulin with her gloved hands and I reached in with tongs for the lobster and then an ear of corn, which I put on the man's plate.

"Looks good enough to eat," Golf Cap said. Everybody was a comedian.

I started to ask Nicki what she meant when Larry came over to us.

"I can't find my gloves anywhere," he said. "You see them?"

We both said no. Everyone who served had a pair of gloves, because the food and the tarpaulin were too hot to touch with your bare hands. Usually at the end of the evening we hung our gloves on hooks inside the cabin.

"Where'd you leave them last?" Nicki asked.

"I hung them up like always," he said.

The last time Larry had worked was the night Kirk was killed.

"You're sure, Larry?" I asked.

"Sure I'm sure. I remember because Bill and Dick and I were hanging our gloves up at the same time. Ask them."

"No need. We believe you. Maybe Dad knows where an extra pair is. Or wait a minute, you could wear Bill's. Or Kirk's."

Larry thought for a moment and then he said, "I'll wear Bill's."

I guessed that it was too painful for him to wear his dead brother's gloves, but on the other hand, why would he rather wear the gloves of someone accused of murdering his brother? I had no answer.

Larry left us and then the parade of people really started. It was lobster and corn time. I could see that I wouldn't be able to really talk to Nicki until our break, when Larry and Charlotte took over for the second seating. It was more than an hour before that happened, but when it did Nicki and I got our sandwiches from the refrigerator in the cabin and sat on the small back porch.

We sat in silence for a bit while I tried to think how Libby Crawford would approach this. I knew Nicki didn't like me, so my asking a lot of questions might tend to put her off. But I didn't know how else to go about it. Just then she interrupted my deliberating.

"Do you think Bill killed Kirk?"

"Of course not," I said, slightly offended.

"I don't either. He's much too kind."

I was surprised she knew that. "I didn't think you knew Bill that well."

"You wouldn't," she said in a snide way.

I wasn't going to let her tone put me off. "What's that mean, Nicki?"

"Nothing." She took a bite of her sandwich and stared past me while she chewed.

That made me mad and suddenly I was blowing my stack. "Listen, Nicki, you've treated me like dirt ever since I got here and I've never known why. Now my brother is in jail for killing your brother and you're acting like . . . like . . . oh, I don't know." I started to cry.

A little time went by and then I felt Nicki's hand on my arm and heard her speak my name. I looked up.

"I'm sorry, Anna," she said. "Please don't cry."

I felt like a real jerk. Here I was blubbering all over the place and it was Nicki who'd had a loss. But then I thought of Bill. I had a right to cry. And for Kirk, too, darn it.

"Nicki," I said, "what's going on?"

"I don't know what you mean."

I took a tissue from my pocket, blew my nose and decided to do my best Libby Crawford imitation: direct questioning!

"Okay, I'll put it to you straight. Why are you acting so weird about Kirk's death?"

Her blue eyes took on a deeper hue, and she straightened up as she moved away from me slightly.

"I don't know what you mean," she said again.

This was really hard, but I had to forge ahead now that I'd started. "I know it's none of my business, but the impression you give is that you don't care that Kirk is dead."

The words hung in the air between us like battle flags. Nicki stared at me, unmoving. I waited. At least a minute passed before she spoke.

"I care very much," she said finally. "I'm glad he's dead."

For a moment I thought I hadn't heard her right, but then I knew I had. Still, I couldn't believe it. And then she went on.

"I hated Kirk!"

I was astonished. I couldn't accept her words.

"I hate Bill sometimes, too, but I—"

"You don't understand," she interrupted. "I didn't

131

hate Kirk sometimes, I hated him *all* the time."

"But why?" I asked.

She looked away from me then, put her half-eaten sandwich down on the brown paper bag.

"I don't want to go into that."

"But you have to, Nicki. You can't just tell me something like that and then not explain."

"Yes, I can," she said simply.

And, of course, she was right. She could say anything she wanted to me. She didn't know I was trying to solve Kirk's murder and that she'd made herself a prime suspect. Her motive was hate, but I very much wanted to know why or how anyone could hate her brother that much.

"Yes, I know you *can*, Nicki, but I wish you'd tell me why."

She turned back to face me, those piercing blue eyes, like Kirk's, boring into mine.

"Because you were in love with him?"

Embarrassment covered me like a second skin, but there was no point in lying to her.

"Yes," I said softly.

"You didn't really know him, Anna."

How many people had said this to me? "I knew him a little bit."

"You knew only what he wanted you to know."

"Isn't that what everyone does? I mean, there are parts of me I don't show to everybody."

She smiled ruefully. "That's not what I mean."

"Well, then, tell me what you mean," I implored.

"You said before that I've treated you like dirt since

132

you got here and I suppose you're right. I knew from the first night what was going to happen between you and Kirk, and I just couldn't be your friend."

"I don't understand. How could you know? What about Charlotte?"

She laughed mirthlessly. "Charlotte was Kirk's doormat. My brother was a rotten person, Anna. He used everyone he came in contact with."

"He didn't use me," I said defensively.

"No?"

"No."

She shrugged. "Maybe he hadn't gotten around to what he wanted from you yet."

"I can't believe this," I said. "Kirk was kind and gentle and, and—"

"Was it kind of him to be fooling around with you behind Charlotte's back?"

I felt tongue-tied. Maybe Nicki knew about Charlotte's breakdown. "He couldn't tell her because of her condition."

"What condition?"

"He was afraid she might have another breakdown."

"You've got to be kidding. Is that what he told you? That Charlotte might have a breakdown if he broke up with her?"

"Like the last one," I said, feeling more feeble with every passing moment.

"What last one?"

"I don't know," I said quietly.

"Listen, Anna, Charlotte never had a breakdown. That was just part of Kirk's game. And you weren't the first girl that he ever fooled around with either. He's been doing it for years. Any new face. I hate to burst your balloon, but you didn't mean any more to Kirk than that," she said, snapping her fingers.

"You don't know that," I said furiously. But I wondered.

Nicki stood up, stuffing her partially eaten dinner back in the bag.

"I *do* know, that's just the trouble. And if I were you I'd forget about Kirk. He's nobody to remember." She started to walk away, but I jumped up and grabbed her arm.

"Wait a minute," I said, "What did you mean when I said that I didn't think you knew Bill that well and you said, 'You wouldn't'?"

"Ask him," she said, and pulled away from me.

I stood my ground while she slammed back into the cabin. I looked at my watch. There were still fifteen minutes left of my break. I sat back down on the step. My appetite was gone, so I packed away the second half of my chicken salad sandwich, got out my notebook and pen and prepared myself to dope this thing out. Whenever Libby Crawford was trying to break a case, she wrote down her ideas on paper. First she made a list of the suspects, and then she wrote notes about each one of them. I would do the same.

1. NICKI
2. LARRY
3. CHARLOTTE
4. DICK

5. WATSON
6. TONY

There were six. My stomach churned. That wasn't quite true. I put my pen to paper.

7. BILL

There were seven.

14

Motive. Means. Opportunity. They were the first three things you had to look for in a murder case, according to Libby Crawford. And I knew that Libby had learned that from my mother, who had learned it from a detective in Maplewood, New Jersey. So if it was good enough for them, it was good enough for me.

Means. It was Kirk's knife, a so-called penknife. Not one of your Swiss Army jobs but an old-fashioned kind with just one blade. One blade six inches long. Long enough to kill. The handle was made of carved ivory, molded in a way that perfectly fit the hand. He always carried it. And he had had it with him the night he was murdered. I knew because I'd seen it.

The night he died, the last night we played the game, there was thunder in the distance.

"Maybe it's going to rain," Larry said. "Maybe we should call it off."

"What's a little rain? Who cares? It'll be fun anyway," Kirk said. He turned his back on the others, looked at me and winked.

I kept a straight face, revealing nothing.

Bill said, "Come on then, let's go."

One by one we went up to the bowl on the table and picked out a piece of paper. When I opened mine it had an M on it. I was to be the murderer. I was glad. It was always fun to be the murderer. And tonight I knew who my victim was going to be.

"I'm the detective," Larry said, waving the paper with a D on it.

He picked up the whistle and hung it around his neck. Then he reached for the stopwatch.

"Everybody ready? One, two, three, go!"

We ran.

There was a lot of thumping of feet and swishing of tall grass as we hurried away.

The moon was only a quarter full, the color of marigolds. It gave very little light, so it was harder than usual to see where you were going. Still, I was able to keep Kirk's form in view, although that wasn't really necessary.

Suddenly I tripped over a branch and cracked it in two. I fell with a thud, grunting as I went down. I hadn't really hurt myself, so I was up quickly. Someone breathing heavily passed me. I thought it was Watson.

I figured that at least a minute had passed. I couldn't

kill until three minutes were up. Wind dashed around me, swirling leaves past my face. The air grew chillier.

And then, to my right in the sky was a streak of lightning. It lasted long enough for me to see Nicki up ahead to my left and Bill right behind her. I couldn't see Kirk, but I knew where he'd gone. We'd arranged it earlier.

The whistle blew, loud and shrill. Everyone stopped. Everyone but me. I made my way through the forest, passing a figure huddled behind a tree. Charlotte, I thought. As I walked I crackled twigs, and in the still of the night the sound was deafening.

Lightning slashed through the sky again. Seconds later I heard the thunder. Again the flash in the sky, this time illuminating everything around me. I saw Dick move from one tree to another. Cheating.

The weather frightened me a little. If lightning hit a tree someone could get hurt. But I didn't have time to think about it. Seconds were ticking away. All in all I had three minutes to find and kill my victim. I'd already used up some of the time.

I hurried to the place that Kirk had designated earlier. He was there, sitting, his back against the tree. I sat beside him.

For a moment I said nothing, and then I took his face between my two hands, turned his head and kissed him on his lips. It was a long, warm kiss and for moments I didn't know where he began and I left off. We merged into one. Then, slowly, I pulled away, put my lips to his ear and whispered: "You're dead."

I had killed him with a kiss.

The second whistle blew.

"A nice way to die," he said. "Can a person be killed twice?"

"I guess it could be arranged," I answered.

We kissed again. This time he put his arms around me and I put mine around him. I felt his hands on my back. One seemed closed in a fist, and something hard was in it. When we parted I traced his arm with my fingers to his hand.

"What's that?" I asked.

"My knife," he said, holding it out on his open palm.

"Why? I mean, what are you going to do with it?"

"I'm going to carve our initials in this tree."

I smiled. That made me happy, corny as it was. "You won't have time," I said.

"If I don't finish, I'll come back tomorrow."

I nodded. "It's time, I think," I said.

"Okay."

He screamed then, and even though I knew it was coming it made me start. He put his arm around me for comfort. We stayed like that a bit and then I knew it was time for me to go back to home base. I rose to my feet as he opened the knife.

"K. C. loves A. P.," he said.

"And A. P. loves K. C. I have to go," I said.

"Right."

Just before I ran I looked at him once more. He'd turned toward the tree, lifting the knife to make his first cut. That was the last time I saw him alive.

It was clear to me now that the moment I'd gone from sight, someone had surprised Kirk, taken the knife from him and stabbed him in the back. Only Bill's fingerprints were on the knife. Bill's and Kirk's. But if the killer had been wearing gloves, then . . . Gloves! Of course. Larry's gloves were missing. The killer *had* worn gloves, I was sure of it. I felt elated for a moment, as though I'd solved the case. And then I realized I wasn't any further ahead than I'd been, because I didn't know *who* had worn them.

But I did know this much: If the murderer *had* worn gloves, it was a premeditated murder. Whoever took those gloves knew what he or she was going to do. Should I, I wondered, tell Smolley about the gloves? I couldn't prove it. It was just a theory, but if I was right it seemed to me that that let Bill off the hook. I had to find out if Bill had used or touched Kirk's knife earlier. He would be home in the morning, and I could ask him then. It seemed to me that if Bill had killed Kirk, he wouldn't have been dumb enough to leave his fingerprints on the knife. After all, he read Mom's books too!

I moved on to Opportunity. That was easy. Everyone had the same opportunity.

Now Motive.

I looked at my list.

Nicki was number one. I wrote her name at the top of a fresh page.

NICKI

She knew her brother always carried a knife, so she would have a weapon at her disposal. Her motive was loud and clear! Hatred. Why did she hate him? Did she hate him enough to kill him? Nicki said she didn't know what she'd do if Bill killed Kirk. What does that mean? If she'd killed Kirk would she say that? Or did she say it to put me off the track? Nicki and Bill a couple? Did Kirk know this and threaten them somehow? If so, then Nicki might have gone over some line. Definitely in the running.

Yes, she was in the running all right, but I had to admit that I had a lot more questions than answers. I went on.

LARRY

Did Larry hate Kirk too? I need to talk to him. Larry's gloves are missing but are they really? Could Larry have taken them himself to kill Kirk and now pretend they are missing to throw suspicion elsewhere?

Suddenly I realized that Larry had not had the same opportunity as the rest of us. He had been the detective, which would have made it much harder to get to Kirk and back again before someone reached home base. Still, I supposed it was possible. I added one more line to my notes on Larry.

Need more info.

CHARLOTTE

Opportunity, yes. She knew about Kirk and me. Definitely jealous. If Nicki is telling the truth then Kirk had cheated on her before. Was I the last straw? Did she love him? Why else put up with his behavior? So why kill *him*? Why not kill me instead?

I swallowed hard. Why not, indeed? And then I realized that it wasn't out of the question for that to happen still. Charlotte had balked at my questioning her; maybe

141

if she realized I was trying to solve the case she *would* kill me. Only, of course, if she was the murderer. If she wasn't and the real murderer found out, then maybe that person would try to kill me. I would have to keep a low profile. But that would be hard to do and investigate at the same time.

Often Libby Crawford got bonked on the head or run off the road or something worse when she was on a case. Still, in the end she triumphed. I smiled. But those were novels, fiction, and this was real life. My smile faded. I went back to my list.

DICK

Kirk's best friend. He seemed eager to get to the bottom of things. Ready to pin it on Tony. So far can't find a motive. Need more info.

WATSON

Clearly didn't like Kirk. The weird exchange he had with Dick. Also, his warning me off. Was he trying to put me off so he wouldn't have to kill me? Be careful of him and get more info.

TONY

He was there during the game but wanted to keep it quiet. Why? Is his reason, that a stranger automatically would be accused, valid? He had a clear motive. Jealousy. He'd seen Kirk and me together . . . kissing. Tony's temper is well known. He could have done it easier than anyone because he had more time. He didn't have to get back to home base. If he was close enough to see Kirk and me in the dark, then he had

142

lots and lots of time. I left; Tony waited a few seconds, then made his move, grabbed the knife and plunged it in Kirk's back. But where were his fingerprints? Could he have had gloves with him? Why? Maybe he wiped off the knife. If so, could Bill's and Kirk's prints have been there? No. Could have used a handkerchief around knife to kill? Awkward. Must be another explanation. Plenty of motive and better opportunity than anyone. High on list.

I shuddered inwardly reading over what I'd written about Tony. And to make it worse I remembered that strange thing he'd said to me the night of the prom: "Don't go hanging yourself now!" That had always given me the willies. And what about the incident in my mini-cave? Had he or hadn't he tried to strangle me? Did I really feel his thumbs pressing on my throat? If Kate hadn't called me just then, what might have happened? I didn't want to think about it but I had to. Tony thought I was the only one who knew when he'd arrived on Blue Haven. If he killed me, then he'd be in the clear. But he loved me, didn't he?

I felt dizzy from all the questions that had no answers. I had one more person on the list, and the time for me to go back to work was growing nearer. I wrote:

Bill

He obviously knows something about Kirk that I don't because of his remark that I wasn't an expert about Kirk. Did he know whatever it was before Kirk was killed? And what about the look Bill exchanged with Watson when Dick said how hard it was to lose a

143

wonderful person like Kirk? Again, the look must have referred to something they knew about Kirk. Something neither Dick nor I knew. Then there is relationship with Nicki. Must find out. And last, the fingerprints. Need more info.

So that was everyone. I read over my notes and put checkmarks next to Nicki's and Tony's names. They were, for the moment, the most likely suspects, with Charlotte right up there. I didn't have enough information about Larry, Dick, Watson and Bill. But I would.

I tucked my notebook and pen back into the front pocket on my overalls and snapped it shut. It wouldn't do at all for me to lose it.

I looked at my watch. I still had a few minutes before I had to go back to work. Now I had to face the things that Nicki had said about Kirk. Kirk and me.

If I believed her, I had to face the fact that Kirk didn't really care for me. That was very hard to swallow. If it was true, he must have been a fantastic actor. I remembered the times we were together, his smile, his touch. Could it all have been pretense? His kisses definitely seemed real. Could you fake kisses like that? Why would anyone want to?

Nicki said that there'd been others. So had Charlotte. *You poor dope. Well, you weren't the first.* The words echoed in my brain. And what about the nervous breakdown that Charlotte was supposed to have had? Obviously it had never happened. This was a lie of Kirk's, made up so that he could keep us both. At least I had to acknowledge this was rotten of Kirk. If he was capable of doing

144

that to Charlotte and to me, I had to accept that he was capable of worse things. Maybe it was true. Maybe I didn't know him at all.

I remembered telling Smolley that everyone liked Kirk and Smolley saying that somebody didn't. Now it seemed that lots of people didn't.

But I didn't know that before he died. No one acted as if they didn't like him. Did Kirk have some power over everyone?

"Oh, there you are," Mom said.

I jumped.

"Nervous Nellie," she said, forcing a smile.

"I didn't hear you," I said.

"Sorry. It's time for you to come back to work."

"I was just coming."

"Could have fooled me," she said.

I stood up. "Mom, what did you think of Kirk?"

"I thought he was a very nice young man. Why do you ask?"

"Nothing. I just wondered." I started past her, but she put a hand on my arm.

"What do you mean, nothing?"

I looked into those big green eyes and wondered if I should tell her some of the things I'd learned about Kirk and maybe get her expert opinion on the matter. But I knew in an instant that it wasn't fair to bother her with my stuff. She had enough to worry about with Bill in jail. And she'd told me herself that her mind was like mush. Still, she'd asked me a question and was waiting for an answer. Easily whirling away from her, I opened the cabin door.

"I'll tell you later, Mom," I said over my shoulder.

But then I heard her calling to me and I stopped and turned to face her.

She came up to me and ran both hands over my hair. "Okay," she said, "you don't have to tell me why you asked if you don't want to. But I just want you to know that, no matter what, I'm here if you need me."

Once again I almost told her but stopped myself. "Thanks, Mom," I said.

She kissed my cheek and went past me, through the cabin and out the front door.

I was more determined than ever to solve this case. I wanted to do it for Mom as well as for Bill. But before I could go any further there was one question that had to be answered. And it was the hardest question I'd ever had to ask!

15

"I'm going to ask you just once, Bill," I said, "and whatever you say I'm going to believe, okay?"

"Okay," he said.

I felt sick about asking but I had to do it. "Did you kill Kirk?"

"No."

"I believe you," I said. "I knew you didn't."

"You know," he said, "while I was in that cell, I thought to myself, if nobody else believes me, I know Anna will."

Smiling at him, I took his hand. We were walking along the beach below our house. It was low tide and the mouth of the bay looked like a mud flat. In the distance the noon sun shone on the water, making it sparkle like ice. Bill had been home only an hour.

"Was it terrible in jail?" I asked.

"Let's put it this way: It's not a nice place to visit and I wouldn't want to live there."

I laughed. "But they weren't mean to you or anything, were they?"

"You've seen too many movies. It was okay, Anna, honest. They brought Tony in, you know."

"I figured as much since he didn't show up last night. He was supposed to come to the restaurant." I wondered if I should tell Bill about my suspicions. I decided it could wait a bit. "They didn't arrest him, did they?"

"No. They just questioned him half the night. There was this one guy, a deputy or something, who kept me informed on what was happening. Al York, nice guy."

"So they let Tony go then?"

"Yeah. But they told him not to leave town. Truth is I don't know why, 'cause they're convinced it was me. At least Smolley is."

"Well he's the only one," I said.

"Thanks, Anna."

"Oh, look." I stopped walking and bent down. A starfish lay on the sand. It was still alive and we watched it move, pulling its five legs in toward the middle. "Make a wish," I said.

"A wish? I never heard of that, making a wish on a starfish."

"So what if you never heard of it? Have you heard of everything in the world?"

He laughed, his nose crinkling and obscuring the few freckles that resided there. He knelt in the sand.

"Okay, I'll make a wish."

"Close your eyes," I instructed.

148

He did.

"Now count to ten, make your wish, then count from ten backwards."

"Give me a break."

"C'mon," I urged.

"I feel like a jerk."

"You *are* a jerk, so what?"

"Thanks, pal. Okay, here I go."

He counted to ten, made his wish silently, then out loud counted from ten to one. His eyes snapped open.

"Will it come true?" he asked.

"Sure."

Looking at me skeptically, he stood up and brushed the sand from his knees. I followed suit and we resumed our walk.

"I guess Tony knows by now that I betrayed him," I said, feeling guilty.

"You didn't betray him, Anna. You *had* to tell. Believe me, I wanted to but I felt it was up to you."

"You're a neat guy," I said.

He pressed his lips together, embarrassed, and looked out at the water.

We walked in silence for a bit; then Bill said:

"Speaking of betrayal, you know why Smolley got interested in me to start with?"

"Why?"

"Somebody told him about my stealing that money."

"Who?" I asked, appalled.

"Who do you think? Peter Hallahan, naturally."

"Are you sure?"

"Sure I'm sure. Who else would it be? I bet he went

right to the police that day he saw us on the street."

"But why, Bill? I mean he didn't know about Kirk or anything."

"So what? You know how that guy is—he just lives to make my life the pits."

I knew Peter Hallahan was mean, but I couldn't believe that he'd take the time on his vacation to go to the police about Bill. Especially when he didn't know what else was going on. Peter was mean but he wasn't dumb. Surely he'd know if he did something like that he'd look bad in the eyes of the police. Of course, if he did know about Kirk's murder then it was possible. I guessed that he could have, because it was in the papers. Still, something about that didn't sit right with me. But now I had another priority.

"Bill," I said, "you and I never really talked about your taking the money."

"I know," he said, looking down at his feet.

"It's my fault."

"Not totally."

"Yes, it is. I was so rotten about the whole thing, how could you have talked to me about it?"

"I guess."

"It's true. I was so wrapped up in how it made me look, I didn't even consider what was going on with you."

"Well, I wasn't exactly taking you into my confidence at the time."

"I don't know why we drifted apart," I said.

"I do. I was angry with you and didn't want to be around you anymore. I couldn't stand it that you were taller than I was."

150

"I should have tried to make you talk to me."

"It wouldn't have worked, Anna. You just would've made me mad."

"Even so I could've tried." He gave my hand a squeeze as if to say he understood. We walked in silence for a bit and then I said, "You know, Bill, the thing I've never understood was how you thought you'd get away with stealing that money."

"Dr. Allen said I did it to get caught. I guess I wanted attention."

"Because of your height?" I asked tentatively.

"In a way. See, the thing is from the time I was in grade school, I thought I'd be some hotshot in sports. Baseball and football mostly."

"I remember. You said you were going to be captain of the Cougars by the time you were a junior."

"Right. So what happens? I end up being the team manager because I'm five feet four. You know how much I envied those guys on the team? It really made me mad that they were out there playing while I was on the sidelines. I guess I was teed off at the guys even though it wasn't their fault I was a shrimp."

"So you stole the money to get back at them."

"Yeah, kind of. But it was really stupid, because stealing that money made me feel about this big." He made a tiny space between his thumb and forefinger.

"How do you feel about it now? Being short, I mean?"

He looked at me and a smile creased his face. "You know, it's funny, I don't care anymore."

I thought I knew why but I didn't want to come on like some know-it-all, so I played it cool.

"That's great, Bill."

"Yeah, great," he said, an edge to his voice. "Out of one jam and into another."

"This one isn't your fault. Listen, getting back to what you told me, who else knew about what you'd done? Watson and Dick and who else?"

Bill shrugged. "I dunno."

"Nicki?" I probed gently.

"Yeah, I guess," he mumbled.

"You told her?"

He nodded.

"Do you think she told Larry?"

"I doubt it," he said defensively.

I smiled to myself, sure now that Bill obviously cared for Nicki. Why hadn't I seen it? I remembered Nicki's words when I said that I didn't think she knew Bill that well. *You wouldn't,* she'd said. Because I was so involved in my romance with Kirk, so involved in *me,* I hadn't seen what was happening between Bill and Nicki.

"Who else knew?" I asked.

"Tony knew," he said.

Tony! But Tony wouldn't have gone to the police voluntarily. He was trying to stay anonymous.

"I don't think he would've gone to the police, do you?"

"No, I don't. Let's sit here, okay?"

We had walked quite a ways and our house was no longer in sight. Now we were near the part of the shore-line where the lobstermen kept shacks to build and mend their traps and to store their skiffs. Each morning they'd come to their shacks and bait their traps with the cut-up, stinky alewives, then row their skiffs out to their

152

powerboats. At this time of day no one was around. Bill and I were alone on the beach.

We sat facing the water, our arms around our bent knees. I noticed first that we were in identical positions.

"Will you just look at us," I said.

"What?"

He saw it then and we both started laughing. And we kept laughing until tears were running down our cheeks. Exhausted, we lay back on the sand, staring up at the sky. It felt wonderful to laugh like that with Bill. It had been an awfully long time. For a while we just stayed that way, not speaking, but enjoying the closeness, the lack of tension. Finally, Bill broke the silence.

"Anna, I asked you once and you wouldn't answer me, but I'm going to ask you again, okay?"

I knew how hard this was for him, so I took him out of his misery. "Yes, Bill, I *was* involved with Kirk."

I heard him expel air as if he'd been holding his breath.

"And you, are you involved with Nicki?"

"Yes."

"Do you love her?"

"I think so."

"I think she loves you," I said.

"I think so, too."

We were having a much easier time talking since we weren't looking at each other but rather staring into the cloudless sky. The sun beat down on us, and I was glad we'd decided to wear bathing suits for our walk.

"Did you love Kirk?" he asked softly.

"I thought I did, but now . . . I have a feeling I didn't

know him at all. You tried to tell me that, didn't you?"

"Yeah. Did he tell you he loved you?"

I remembered K.C. loves A.P. but I didn't think that's what Bill meant. "Well, he never actually said it, but he told me he didn't love Charlotte."

"He didn't love anybody, Anna. He couldn't."

"Why do you say that?"

"Because he was a rotten person."

My first instinct was to tell Bill to shut up, but I knew I had to listen to what he had to say.

"How? How was he rotten?"

"Well, for one thing the way he treated Charlotte. Didn't you ever think about that?"

That made me mad and I sat up and looked down at him. "Listen, Bill, don't try and lay a guilt trip on me, okay?"

He sat up, too. "I'm sorry. I shouldn't have said that."

"But if you must know, yes, I thought about it a lot. The thing was, I felt I was in love with him and he seemed to feel the same about me so I didn't know what to do. Then he told me that Charlotte had had a break-down and that he couldn't tell her about us because she might go to pieces."

"What a creep," Bill said. "Charlotte never had any breakdown."

"I know that now. Nicki told me. Bill, why did Nicki hate Kirk so much?"

A look of pain infused his brown eyes. "You'd better ask her," he said.

"I did but she wouldn't tell me. Do you know?"

154

"Yes." He clenched and unclenched his fists. "It makes me so mad just to think about it."

"Please tell me, Bill."

He ran his hand through his hair, then back down over his face as if he was wiping away his anger. But it still showed clearly when his hand fell to his chest.

"Okay, Anna, but you can't tell anybody. I mean like Smolley or anyone."

"Smolley? Why would I tell him?"

"I dunno. I'm just saying, okay?"

"I swear, Bill, honest."

"Okay. Well, last year . . . last year Kirk made Nicki pose for him and he took a whole bunch of pictures."

I waited for him to go on but that was all. At first I didn't understand, didn't get the implication of what Bill had said, and then slowly it dawned on me.

"You mean . . . naked pictures?"

"Yeah."

"I don't believe it," I said automatically.

"It's true."

"But why did she do it?"

"He threatened her."

"With what?" I couldn't imagine any threat that would make me do that.

"You have to understand that Kirk's always been the favorite of the Cunninghams and that whatever he said or did they went along with. They thought he was perfect."

So did I, I thought. "He was very convincing."

"Yeah, I guess. Anyway, he used to beat Nicki up—

155

with a rubber hose so there wouldn't be any marks. Early on she told her mother, but she didn't believe her so Nicki knew that wasn't an option. Telling her parents. Anyway, Kirk threatened her with more beatings if she didn't pose for him."

I felt shocked. "But why had he been beating her to start with?"

"For fun."

"I can't believe this, Bill, I just can't."

"He was a sick guy, Anna. You don't understand. You know what he did with the pictures? He sold them to guys at college. Can you imagine? His own sister."

All the warmth I'd felt from being close to Bill drained away and in its place was a hollowness. Part of me wanted to believe that Bill was making this up or that Nicki had, but in the depths of me I knew it was true. I thought I might be sick. Standing up, I said, "Let's go for a swim." I wanted the water to wash away everything I'd heard.

We ran into the water, going out yards and yards before it was swimmable. Maine water is cold but it felt good, numbing me to everything but it. Both of us are excellent swimmers, so we headed back toward the house, side by side. After some time Bill said he was getting out and I followed.

We walked in silence, each with our own pain. The water had washed away nothing. Finally, I said, "What about Larry? Did he hate Kirk too?"

"Yeah."

"Why?"

"I don't know. Nicki doesn't know either."

I would have to speak to Larry, find out more. For now I had to concentrate on Bill. I wanted to know about the fingerprints on the knife.

"Bill, how did your fingerprints get on Kirk's knife?" I asked.

"That's easy. I borrowed it from him that night on my break."

"What for?"

"Do I have to tell you, Anna?" He nervously pulled at his chin.

"I can't make you tell me," I said.

"It's embarrassing."

"Oh, Bill. I won't laugh or put you down or anything."

"Well, okay. I borrowed it so I could cut Nicki's and my initials in the big spruce behind the cabin at the restaurant. Corny, huh?"

His words were like a punch in the stomach. "Did Kirk know that's why you wanted it?"

"Yeah, the creep. I didn't tell him, but he followed me out there, spied on me, you know, and then when I got it all done he jumped out from behind another tree and started laughing and making fun of me. It was totally obnoxious."

"I can imagine," I said flatly. So that was where Kirk had gotten the idea to carve our initials. What a dope I'd been. "Did you tell Smolley that you'd borrowed the knife?"

"Sure. You think I'm a jerk? Never mind, don't answer that. Anyway, I told him. I even had to tell him why. But he didn't believe it. See, I couldn't prove it

157

'cause no one else knew. I'd done it as a surprise for Nicki, so she didn't even know. All I had was my word, which isn't too hot with Smolley."

"But the initials are there in the tree," I said excitedly.

"So? That proves *nada*. I could have done that anytime with any knife."

I felt deflated.

"But a funny thing is that there are only two prints of mine on the knife. The deputy, Al York, told me. And he also said that the rest of the knife was smudged like somebody had wiped it or worn gloves."

I stopped. "Worn gloves? He actually said that?"

"Yeah, why? What's the big deal?"

"The big deal is that I think somebody *did* wear gloves." I told him about Larry and the missing gloves and what my theory was.

"So maybe we should look for those gloves," he said.

"A good idea. Tonight. After we close. We'll tell Mom and Dad we're just going for a ride, and then when everyone's gone we'll come back."

"Okay. I'm not sure what we can prove if we find them, but it might help. You don't think we should tell Smolley to look for them, do you?" he asked.

"Do you?"

"Nah. He'd laugh at us."

"Right."

So Bill and I were partners. It felt good. When we got back to the house, I decided to tell him everything I knew and to show him my notebook. I would tear out the page about him but show him the rest and see what he thought.

158

"Meet me in my room in ten minutes," I said. "I have something to show you."

"Okay."

We started for the back door, but Bill stopped me before I opened it.

"One question," he said.

"Shoot."

"That starfish wish stuff back there—you just made it up, didn't you?"

"You'll never know," I said, and scurried past him into the house.

I had, of course, but you never knew what might work, and Bill needed all the help he could get.

16

Driving toward Cranberry Harbor I noticed once again that the houses were oddly shaped. This was true in a great part of Down East Maine. They were either tall and narrow or short and squat. Some had cornices that knocked your eyes out and others had porches that were in odd places, making them useless. Some houses were painted white but others were fire-engine red or turquoise, maybe a yellow the color of saffron. A few were blue and one was a luscious lavender.

I made my turn into town. The streets were quiet. It was only eight in the morning. Occasionally I passed someone carrying a newspaper or a white paper bag that obviously held jelly doughnuts or sugar buns. The majority of stores didn't open until ten, and most people were still asleep, on vacation.

After I had shown my notebook to Bill, and we had

again discussed the missing gloves and deliberated over who had told about his theft, we agreed that we should put off our search until I could go to Smolley with a trade. There hadn't been time until this morning. If Smolley would tell me who had squealed about Bill, then I would give him the information about the gloves. Bill wanted to come with me, but we realized that he wasn't in any position to bargain, and the less Smolley saw of him the better.

I had gotten up before the others and crept out of the house. Mom and Dad wouldn't notice that I was gone until they went outside and saw that my car was missing. Bill would tell them then that I'd gone shell hunting with Nicki. I wasn't sure Mom would buy that one, because she was a pretty observant person and it wouldn't have taken much to notice that Nicki and I were not what you might call chums. Still, it was the best we could come up with, and if my parents didn't believe me I'd deal with it later.

The police station in Cranberry Harbor was on Seawall Street, which was off the main drag. It was a red-brick building, low and ugly. I parked my car a few yards down and walked back. I didn't know if Smolley would be in so early, but I planned to wait until he did come in. I had a book with me to pass the time if that was necessary.

The double doors were heavy (so crooks couldn't break in?) and I had to push with all my weight to gain entrance. Almost immediately in front of me was a high desk with a policeman behind it. He was younger than I would have expected and had dry-looking brown hair and pop eyes. He reminded me of a puppet I'd had as a child.

"C'n I help you, Miss?"

"I'm looking for Detective Smolley."

"Detective Smolley," he repeated.

"Yes. Is he in?"

"Ay-uh."

There was that sound again. Surely it meant yes. I took a chance. "May I see him, please?"

"Who should I say is inquirin'?"

"Anna Parker."

He nodded, lifted a phone and pushed a button. "Sir, a young lady's out heah and wishes to see ya. Anna Pahka. Yes, sir." He replaced the phone and looked at me, his pop eyes resembling two painted Ping-Pong balls. "Ya can go in now. Fust doah on youh right."

I thanked him and followed his directions. At the door I didn't know whether to knock or walk in so I knocked.

"Ay-uh?" Smolley said from within.

Could that mean I should enter? I opened the door and went in.

Harvard Smolley was sitting behind a metal desk in a short-sleeved shirt that was open at the neck. "Mawnin', Anna."

"Good morning," I said.

"Nice ta see ya. Sit down. You must be a mind reada."

I was puzzled and frowned.

"I was gonna come up ta youh house in anotha hour or so to see ya, but ya beat me to it."

I sat in a hard metal chair facing him. "Why were you going to come see me?"

162

"Well, I reckon the same reason you've come heah."

Could he know about the gloves or that I wanted to know who'd told him about Bill? I decided to play it very cool. "And what's that?" I asked.

"Tony Nardone, I reckon."

"Oh. Him."

Now Smolley had a puzzled look on his face. "Oh. Him," he imitated. "I thought Mr. Nardone was youh boyfriend."

I felt my mouth begin to twitch in annoyance. "He was. Not anymore."

"I see. But ya do know him?"

"Sure." I didn't like the way things were going. It seemed like the old table-turning routine. "Mr. Smolley, I didn't come here to talk about Tony."

"Well, now," he said, and leaned back in his chair, which creaked and groaned under his weight.

I waited for him to ask me why I *had* come, but soon I could tell he wan't going to so I went on.

"I wanted to make a deal with you," I said.

He arched an eyebrow. "Oh? What kind of deal?"

"I have some information that might be important pertaining to the murder of Kirk Cunningham, and you have some information that is important for me to know. I thought we could make a trade."

"A trade, huh? Mighty interestin', mighty interestin'." He stroked his mustache with his forefinger and thumb as he rocked in his chair. "What would the trade be, exactly?

"I want to know who told you about Bill stealing the money last year."

163

"Ay-uh. And what's youh part?"

"Well, I can't tell you that until you tell me."

"Ay-uh." He pursed his lips, scratched his cheek, ran a hand through his light-brown hair and rubbed his nose. "Well, now, deah, I don't think we can make this heah deal. It wouldn't be right, ya unduhstand? But ya can do me a favah and tell me what time Tony Nardone got to Blue Haven."

I didn't know if Smolley was trying to trick me or not, but I wasn't about to lie anymore for Tony.

"I can only tell you what he told me and the time I first saw him."

"Good enough."

"Tony said he got to the restaurant about nine-thirty, just as we were starting the game." I hoped Tony had told the truth, because if he hadn't he was going to be in a lot of trouble now. "And he was hiding in my closet when I went up to bed. That was after midnight."

Smolley nodded as if what I'd said tallied with his information, but his nod might not have meant that at all.

"Tell me," he said, "did Tony know about you and Kirk?"

I was shocked. Somebody had been talking about me. But why not? There was no reason to be surprised. I'd talked to Smolley about the others—why should I expect that they wouldn't talk about me? It had probably been Nicki.

"Anna?" he said.

"Yes, Tony knew. He found out that night."

"Is he the jealous type?"

164

"Yes." I felt like a rat. I was practically putting Tony behind bars. Still, I couldn't say he was innocent, that he absolutely and positively didn't do it, because I had wondered myself.

"Do you think Tony's capable of killin'?" Smolley asked.

I certainly didn't want to answer that one, nor did I think I had to. I'd been more than cooperative so far. Now it was his turn. But it was clear to me that Smolley wasn't going to tell me, no matter what, who had spilled the beans about Bill. I would have to find out another way. What would Libby Crawford do? I wondered.

"Ya heah me, Anna?"

"I heard and I don't think it's very fair of you to ask me to speculate about something like that."

"Guess not," he said agreeably.

I wasn't getting anywhere with what I wanted to know. How to do it? Libby Crawford would try and trick Smolley in a situation like this, I remembered.

"Course it wouldn't be exactly speculation if you'd ever seen the fella nasty or violent or somethin'," he said.

I had it.

"Well, Mr. Smolley, if you wanted to know about that, you should have asked Peter Hallahan when he came in."

"Who?"

My heart almost stopped.

"Peter Hallahan."

Smolley leaned forward and picked up a pen. "Spell it."

I did.

"Who's Peter Hallahan?"

It was obvious to me now that Peter hadn't been the one who had told Smolley about Bill. So it had to be one of the other five. Who wanted to incriminate Bill? And why?

Very innocently I said, "Oh, I thought you knew Peter. Somebody told me you'd called him in for questioning." I hoped you couldn't get in trouble for lying to an officer of the law the way you could in court.

"Nevah heard of him. Who is he?"

So now I was about to get Peter in hot water. Well, so what? He deserved it after all the humiliation he'd put Bill through.

"Peter's from our old town. An outlander, as you call us. He's vacationing here. At least he was a few days ago."

Smolley looked interested. "Was he heah the night of the murdah?"

I shrugged. "Don't know."

"You know where he's stayin'?"

"Nope. I saw him here, though."

"In Cranberry Hab-ba?"

"Yup."

"And ya say that he would know a lot about Tony Nardone?"

I swallowed. Another lie. Well, an equivocation. "He might." Maybe he did. They played football together, after all.

"I'll look into this," he said.

"Good." I knew I had to go back to my original plan, ask Smolley again about a deal, or else he'd know I'd

166

tricked him. Besides, if there was any hope of him telling who *did* report Bill, then I wanted to know. I was positive now that that person had incriminated Bill because he or she was the guilty one.

"Mr. Smolley, won't you tell me who told you about Bill stealing the money?"

"Can't do that, Anna."

"I think it's very important."

"How so?"

"I think whoever told you is probably the real killer. I mean, why would somebody do that for no reason?"

Smolley lit his third cigarette since I'd been there. "Well, now, I can think of lots of reasons."

"Name one."

He smiled, looking like a boy. "One, huh? Okay. One would be that the puhson wanted to help the police with their investigation and nothin' more. One would be because the puhson was honest and truthful and when the police officer asked did the puhson know of any other puhson who'd ever been in trouble before, that puhson didn't want to lie. Like some people."

Did he mean me?

"Now then, what's this infuhmation you had?" he asked.

I had no intention of telling him about the gloves now that we weren't going to make a trade.

"I just made that up," I said.

The eyebrow again. "You mean, you lied to a police officeh?"

It seemed either way, telling or not, I was in a bind. "It wasn't really a *lie*," I said, trying to sound cheerful.

"No?"

167

"It was a trick. I played a trick on you, that's all." Now I was telling the truth. Of course Harvard Smolley didn't know which trick I was referring to. I stood up. "That's all it was, a trick that failed." A lie again. I had to get out of here.

He stood up, too. "Mind if I give you a piece of advice?"

I shrugged.

"I think you should leave the police work to me and the otha officehs."

"I don't know what you mean."

"Oh, I just thought you might have a mind to go diggin' around, pokin' into things you shouldn't ought to be pokin' into. Like who told me what. Business like that."

"I did think it was important," I said.

"'Tisn't."

"I guess not. Well, thanks for seeing me."

"Anytime, anytime."

He walked me to the door and opened it. I turned then and looked into his clear blue eyes. I had to ask one more question.

"Mr. Smolley, do you really think my brother killed Kirk Cunningham?"

He took a long drag of his cigarette, held it, blew a stream of gray smoke past me into the hall and tapped his foot several times.

"Well, now, Miss Pahka, I know it's hard to believe youh own brother could kill someone, but I do, indeed, think he did it."

"But what evidence do you have?"

168

"Theah's the fingerprints and the haih."

"The what?"

"Haih," he said pointing to the hair on his head.

"What hair?"

"A couple of red haihs were found on the body."

"Well, that was probably *my* hair," I blurted out.

"Ay-uh, mebbe. We'll know bettah when we get the lab tests back from Boston."

"So that's why you asked me how I wore my hair when you questioned me."

"Ay-uh."

I knew for sure now that Smolley *never* asked unnecessary questions.

"Okay, so you have two lousy prints and some hair that may be Bill's or may be mine. Pretty flimsy. What motive have you got?"

"Mebbe he didn't like his sister foolin' around with Kirk and mebbe he didn't like his girlfriend puttin' up with Kirk. Theah's two right theah."

So he knew about Kirk and Nicki. I wondered what else he knew about Kirk, but I realized he'd never tell me.

"You just don't know my brother," I said. "He'd never kill anyone, no matter what."

"If I had a nickel for every time I heahd somebody say that about a killer, I'd be a rich man."

"But it's true about Bill."

"It's always true," he persisted.

This was a dead end, I could see. So I said good-bye and left the situation.

Outside I sat in my car thinking. So far, Nicki, Char-

169

lotte, Tony and even Bill had motives for killing Kirk. And according to Bill it seemed like Larry did, too. I'd have to talk with him to find out for sure. Watson and Dick were left. And they were the two I was sure knew about Bill and the money. I looked at my watch. Soon Watson would be coming back after hauling his traps. I knew where his shack was, so I decided to go there and wait for him.

One thing I was going to do for sure was to ask each person right out whether he or she had told Smolley about Bill's theft. I would do it in such a way that the person wouldn't be embarrassed by having told Smolley. I'd be understanding and sympathetic. Then if somebody admitted it, I'd ask why and at least be able to put that theory to rest. But if *nobody* admitted it, then I'd have to go back to my original idea: Whoever told Smolley was the real killer.

I started the car. Watson Hayden, I thought, you'd better be in an honest mood today, because here comes Anna Parker, major sleuth!

17

Watson's shack was no different from any of the others dotting the shore. The door was unlocked so I went in. The smell of fish was almost overpowering, but I knew that in a minute or so I'd get used to it.

There wasn't much inside: a few traps, a wooden chair, a set of oars, some buckets and netting, a set of black-and-yellow waders, a metal fishing box.

A few weeks before I had read a book about lobstering, so I knew all about lobster traps and how hard the fishermen work.

Watson's lobster traps, like most others, were made of bent saplings and laths. Flat rocks were what he used on the bottoms for weight. Some fishermen used cement slabs. The buoys, connected to the traps by long nylon lines, were air-blown plastic that floated on the surface of the water. Net bags were used to hold the bait and

171

were put inside the traps. Then they were dropped overboard, where they sank to the bottom. A few days later the fisherman would ride out in his motorboat to where a buoy was, hook it up to his winch, which was connected to his motor, and haul in the trap. With any luck it would hold a bunch of lobsters as well as other small creatures, seaweed and any old thing that happened to get caught.

Being a lobster fisherman was a hard life. A life, I knew, that Watson didn't want. I remembered Smolley asking me if Watson was angry about not being able to go to college. I'd been rather flip in my answer, saying something like "wouldn't you be?" But the truth was I didn't really know what he felt about it. I'd just taken Kirk's word for it, and now I didn't know if I could believe anything Kirk had said.

I sat down on the rickety wooden chair, unsnapped the front pocket of my overalls and took out my notebook and pen. Riffling the pages, I soon found my notes on Watson. When I read them over I felt a bit frightened. Everything I'd written made him sound very suspicious and maybe even dangerous. Maybe it was dumb to have come here, maybe I should . . .

A dark shadow fell across my notebook and I raised my head. Startled, I jumped up and looked into the face of Watson Hayden. He was frowning, his lips a white slash in his face.

"What are you doing here?" he asked angrily.

"Gee," I said, trying to lighten things up, "it's great to be greeted so nicely."

"Ah, well," he muttered, and nervously ran his palm

172

over his crew cut. "Just meant, you know, how come you're here, that's all."

"I came for that talk."

"What talk?"

"Remember when I dropped you off at your house I asked you if we could have a talk some other time? Well, this is it."

"Excuse me," he said, pushing past me and sitting down on the chair, where he began to take off his waders. "I recollect that I said on that occasion there was nothing to talk about. What's that you got there?"

"Huh?"

He pointed to my notebook, which I'd forgotten I was holding. "Oh, nothing," I said, and quickly stuffed it into my front pocket."

"Looks like something to me." His wet waders off, he slipped into his extra pair.

"I was just sketching," I said.

"You draw?" His eyes behind the glasses seemed to grow wide with wonder. "Lemme see." He stood up and moved closer to me, his hand outstretched.

Now what had I done? "No, I'd rather not. They're not very good."

"That's okay. I'd like to see them. I draw, too, don'tcha know," he said shyly.

I was surprised. I guess I'd put Watson in some sort of niche and it didn't include the arts. It just showed how wrong you could be about people when you judged them on the surface. The way I had with Kirk.

"Will you show me your drawings?" I asked.

"I'm no good. I just fool around." He smiled with his lips instead of his whole face.

I noticed, not for the first time, that Watson had a sweet look to him sometimes. If he didn't cut his hair that way, if he'd let it grow, he might have had a less pinched look about him. He might have even been cute. I wished I knew him better so I could tell him.

"I'd still like to see your drawings," I said.

"And I'd like to see yours."

I realized that I shouldn't have pursued seeing his drawings, because now I'd have to tell the truth about my notebook. I was trapped.

"These aren't drawings, Watson. I just said that." I shrugged helplessly.

"How come?"

"I don't know. It was the first thing that came into my head."

"You making fun of me?" he asked warily.

"Oh, no. I had no idea that you drew. Honest." I made a cross over my heart with my forefinger.

"Well, then, what's in that notebook?"

"Notes."

"About what?"

Suddenly I remembered a Libby Crawford case where she let all the suspects know she suspected them, hoping to force someone's hand. It had worked, but Libby had nearly been poisoned. Oh, well nothing ventured, nothing gained!

"About everybody," I said.

"Like who?" He took off his glasses and slowly wiped them on his T-shirt.

"Like Nicki and Charlotte, Larry, Dick, Tony and you."

"How come?"

"I'm trying to figure out who killed Kirk," I said simply.

He looked surprised. "Oh, yeah? And have you?"

"Not yet. But I will."

Watson shook his head then put his glasses back on. "Listen, Anna, you better not mess around or you might get hurt."

"Is that a warning or a threat?" I asked.

A hurt look crossed his face as if I'd said something really terrible. "A warning, naturally. Why would I threaten you?"

"I don't know," I said. "Will you answer some questions?"

"What kind of questions?"

It had occurred to me that maybe I'd do better if I asked the person I was talking to about the others. After all, nobody was going to purposely incriminate himself.

"Some questions about Dick, for instance."

"Dick," he said sullenly.

"You don't like him?"

"Not much."

"Why not?"

"He was Kirk's yes man, if you take my meaning. Listen, can we get out of here?"

"Sure."

We walked outside and Watson led us to his truck.

"Gotta make some deliveries. You wanna come?"

"Okay."

I climbed up into the passenger side of the truck.

"Where's your car?" he asked.

"I parked it up farther."

"I'll bring you back here before I deliver to your folks, okay?"

"Perfect," I said.

He started the engine and we huffed our way up the winding dirt road.

"So," I said, "you don't like Dick because he was Kirk's yes man?"

"Right. He was supposed to be Kirk's best friend, but I sure wouldn't be like that with my best friend."

"Be like what?"

"Well, now, if I had a best friend who did stuff like Kirk, I'd sure come down on him. But Dick, he just sat by, saying nothing, doing nothing. I have no respect for a fella like that."

"What kind of things did Kirk say and do?"

"You sure you want to know?" He glanced at me a moment and I could see he was genuinely concerned.

"Yes, I'm sure."

"Look, I know you were . . . well, hanging around with Kirk, so maybe there are things you wouldn't want to know."

I had to face it. Everybody had known about Kirk and me. Had Nicki told everyone?

"How'd you know about that?" I asked.

"See, this is just what I mean." He chewed on his lower lip.

"What is?"

"You finding out stuff that maybe you shouldn't."

"Please, Watson, it's important that you tell me."

We drove in silence for a bit and then he nodded once as if he'd been having a conversation with himself and had made a decision.

"Okay," he said, "okay. But don't say I didn't warn you."

"I won't."

"Well, I knew 'cause Kirk told me. He told everybody, Anna."

A feeling of pain coursed through me. "But why?"

"Don't know how to say this so you won't be all shook up, so I guess I'll just have to say it right out. He wanted us all to know he'd . . . well, gotten you. Know what I mean?"

I swallowed hard, fighting back tears. "You mean like a notch on his belt."

"That's it," he said softly, "that's right. He told everything that went on between you two and some stuff that probably didn't, I reckon. And Dick Beal, he just sat there like a mummy letting him say more and more. That's why I don't like Dick. He condoned everything Kirk did. Leastways, it seemed like that to me. Made me damn mad, I'll tell you."

"Mad enough to kill him?" I asked.

The truck swerved and we almost went off the road, but Watson got it back under control right away.

"Hey, what a thing to say. Course not. I admit I didn't like that sucker, but I wouldn't kill him. I gotta stop here for a delivery."

He pulled over and killed the motor. Before he got out, he reached under the seat and pulled out a tattered portfolio.

"Here," he said, "you can look at these while I'm gone. Don't laugh too hard." He slammed shut the driver's door and I found myself alone with his drawings.

I undid the string and carefully opened it up. I was stunned by the first one. It was a pencil drawing of a fisherman and it was wonderful. Watson was a terrific artist. I quickly turned to the next one. A water scene with birds. Excellent. I kept going through them and each one was as good if not better than the last. And then my heart almost stopped.

I had turned over a portrait. It was hideous. Not the execution—that was as good as the others—but the content, the face. And even though it was ugly and evil-looking, I could still see that it was Kirk. My hands began to shake and my breathing came in little, short rasps. I'd never seen anything so horrible. The feeling of malevolence practically jumped off the paper.

Suddenly the door on my side was wrenched open. Watson, out of breath as if he'd been running, stood there looking down at Kirk's portrait.

"Oh, God," he said.

I didn't know what to say. I just looked from him back to the drawing, then back to him again.

"I . . . I forgot that was in there . . . then . . . I . . . I remembered."

"It's horrible," I said.

"I know. But that's how *he* was." He grabbed the portfolio from me and slammed shut the door.

I sat still, staring straight ahead. I heard Watson enter the truck but I couldn't look at him.

"Listen, Anna, you just don't understand."

"Then explain," I said.

"I told you, he was no good. Oh, he fooled people all right. On the surface he seemed gentle and kind and sensitive, but he wasn't. Something was really wrong with him. He just liked to use people, hurt them. Don't know anybody that guy didn't hurt. 'Cept adults, teachers and the like."

I decided to use this opening. I turned toward him and said, "How did he hurt Larry?"

"Not sure, but I know he did. Kirk had some kind of hold over that kid, 'cause Larry jumped every time Kirk asked him to do something. But Larry hated him."

"How do you know?"

"Heard him tell Kirk he did. Was the night of the murder, in fact."

"What? What did you hear?" I asked excitedly.

"It was when I came over to the restaurant that night. Had to use the bathroom, so I went on into the cabin. When I opened the bathroom door I could hear them arguing. They were behind the metal partition and didn't hear me come in, don'tcha know? Anyway I heard Larry say he wouldn't do it and then Kirk told him he'd better if he knew what was good for him, but Larry just kept saying he wouldn't. Then Kirk said if he didn't he'd tell about last summer. Larry yelled that maybe Kirk wouldn't have the chance. Then I heard a scuffle like, and Larry yelled, 'I hate you, Kirk, I hate your guts and I wish you were dead.' "

Larry was moving up the suspects list pretty fast. "What did Kirk say?" I asked.

"Didn't say anything, he just laughed. Then Larry

came running past me, but he didn't see me, he was crying too hard."

"Do you think Larry could have killed Kirk?"

"Maybe. Don't know. Don't care. If he did, so what?"

"I'll tell you what," I said angrily. "My brother is being accused of the murder, that's what."

"Oh yeah. Forgot about that."

"And speaking of Bill," I said, "did you tell Smolley Bill had stolen money in Maplewood?"

"Course not, Anna. What do you think I am, some kind of stool pigeon?"

"Well, somebody did."

"Not me."

I believed him. "I just wish I knew who did, because I think whoever did killed Kirk. Who could have hated him that much?"

"Listen, Anna, everybody hated Kirk, so it could have been anybody."

"Dick too?"

"Ask him."

"Come on, Watson, tell me."

"Don't know. He always acted like he worshiped Kirk, but who knows?"

"I still don't see why you hated Kirk so much. I mean, was there some personal hatred between you?"

Watson looked away as he started up the truck. "Think I'd better take you back to your car," he said.

I knew that he wasn't about to answer any more questions so I kept silent on the ride back. When we reached my car he pulled over and cut the motor.

"I'm worried 'bout you, Anna," he said. "A person

who kills once isn't scairt of killing twice, you know."

Again I wondered if this was a warning or a threat, but I didn't ask. I just looked at him.

"Okay," he said. "Okay. You wanna know why I hated Kirk, I'll tell you. Somebody else is bound to anyways. He took my girl away from me, that's why."

"Was it someone like me? I mean, was she just another notch on his belt?" I asked.

"Yeah, a big one. I wouldn't have minded so much if he'd really loved her, but he never did. He just didn't like me having a girl. Kirk never wanted anybody to have anything. Wanted it all for himself even if he didn't care for the person or the thing. That's why I hated him."

"Did you ever try and get your girl back? After he dropped her?" I asked.

"He never dropped her. It was Charlotte."

I was astonished. Charlotte! Charlotte had been Watson's girl once. Once, before Kirk had come along and stolen her away.

"I'm sorry," I said. "I really am."

"Thanks," he mumbled, and put his head down on the steering wheel.

I didn't know if he was going to cry or not, but I knew if he did he'd be embarrassed if I was around. I opened the door and got out.

When I was pulling away in my car I looked back and saw that he was still in the same position. And as sorry for him as I was, I hadn't lost my objectivity.

Watson Hayden had just climbed to the number-one spot on the suspect list.

181

18

I made a date to have an early lunch with Dick Beal at a place called The Hollywood Cafe in Cranberry Harbor. I don't know why it was called that except all the sandwiches were named after movie stars. It was very dumb but the food was good.

I got there early so that I could be involved in my notebook when he arrived. I saw him come in, but I remained bent over my work, writing intently.

"Diary?" he asked, sitting down opposite me.

I jumped slightly, and quickly closed the book, pretending he'd caught me at something.

"Hi, Dick."

"Hi. What were you doing?"

"Oh, nothing. Just working on a few ideas."

"Ideas? Ideas for what?"

"Well, that's why I wanted to have lunch, so we could discuss them."

"You've lost me, Anna." He smiled, and his small eyes got smaller.

I leaned into the table and whispered, "About the murder."

"Oh." His smile faded and he took on a serious, businesslike air. "Do you have some special ideas?" he asked, pointing to the notebook.

I pulled it closer to me and covered it with both hands as if it contained important secrets. "I have *some* ideas, but I wanted to hear yours."

"I'm not sure I understand."

The waitress interrupted us then. I ordered a Richard Gere, which was turkey, chopped chicken livers and fried onions on rye. Dick ordered a Brooke Shields. That was roast beef, turkey, cole slaw and Russian dressing on pumpernickel. Idly I wondered if either of those stars liked those kinds of sandwiches or whether the management had simply made them up. What I hated most about it was having to order by name. It made me feel like a jerk to have to say "I'll have a Richard Gere," but what could you do?

When the waitress left, Dick repeated that he didn't know what I was talking about.

"I thought maybe you had some ideas as to who murdered Kirk. If I remember correctly, you thought about trying to solve it yourself."

He ran two fingers down the bridge of his large nose as if he were making a crease. "Well, that was, I don't

183

know, I guess it was in the heat of the moment or something. How would I know what to do, where to begin? Anyway, I hate to remind you, Anna, but your brother's already been charged with it, hasn't he?"

His words made me mad, but I kept my feelings in check. "That doesn't mean he did it," I said evenly.

"Of course not." He toyed with his fork, twirling it through his fingers like a miniature baton.

"Do *you* think Bill did it?"

He shrugged. "Well, I don't know. I feel like you're putting me on the spot here. I mean, I don't really know Bill, do I?"

"I guess not. By the way, did you mention to Smolley about Bill stealing that money last year?"

"I didn't even know about it when Smolley questioned me," he said easily.

I decided to skip pointing out that he could have told Smolley later, because if Dick *had* told he wasn't about to admit it. Who would? It was dumb to keep asking people about it.

"I've found out some interesting things since the last time we talked," I said.

"Yeah, like what?"

"Oh, this and that." I tapped my notebook as if it was an unconscious gesture.

"Well, aren't you going to tell me? I mean, what's the point of this meeting if you aren't going to share your insights with me?"

"I guess you're right. I suppose I could tell you *some* things," I said, and put my notebook into my front pocket, snapping it shut.

184

"Like what?"

"Like . . ."

The waitress came with our food and drinks and set them down in front of us. I was starving because I hadn't had any breakfast. I picked up half of my Richard Gere and bit a huge piece out of the center. Delicious. Dick just stared at me while I chewed. I gestured toward his Brooke Shields, and he picked up a half with very little enthusiasm.

"Good," I mumbled.

He took a small bite and put the sandwich back on the plate. He finished chewing before I did.

"Are you going to tell me or what?" he asked.

I nodded, swallowed, took a sip of my Tab and wiped my mouth with my napkin. "Sure thing," I said. I told him what I'd learned about Larry's fight with Kirk and asked him what he thought it might be about.

"Beats me," he said, shrugging his bony shoulders. "But I can tell you this, Larry worshiped his brother. If he really said something like that, well, we all say things we don't mean, don't we?"

I thought of the times I'd said things in anger to Bill and Kate. "Sure we do."

"Anyway, it seems to me Larry's the one person who couldn't have done it no matter what."

"What do you mean?"

"Well, he was the detective. He had to stay at home base. There just wasn't enough time."

This wasn't news to me, but I didn't want to let go of the idea that Larry might have done it. "Well, maybe. On the other hand, right after he blew the second whistle he could've found Kirk, waited until I left, come out of hiding, killed him and run back. I admit it would be cutting it pretty close, but it could be done."

"When you got back to home base who was there?"

"I was the first one. Except for Larry. He was there."

"So let me understand this. After Kirk screamed, Larry waited nearby for two minutes until you left, then killed Kirk and got back to home base before you did. Is that what you're saying, Anna?"

"Right. He could've done it. He's a fast runner, you know."

Dick shook his head. "Seems unlikely."

"Who says he had to blow the second whistle from home base?"

"Well, we would've heard the difference, wouldn't we, Anna?"

"Maybe." I took another bite of my sandwich. In New Jersey they made the same sandwich but with chicken fat. I missed that. "I still think it could be done." I wasn't concentrating on Larry now. Something was bothering me but I didn't know what. I felt as though I'd missed something important, a link or connection. I quickly tried to review our conversation, but whatever it was eluded me now.

"I suppose it could be done, but boy oh boy, what a chance to take. I can't buy it." He dug into his sandwich with more gusto than before.

"I guess you're right," I said, but I wasn't convinced. I wanted to move on to the others.

We took them one by one, Nicki, Charlotte, Watson and Tony, and with each person Dick tried to show me why or how they couldn't have done it. I didn't think he made a good case for any of them, and by the time we finished our sandwiches and ordered coffee, I felt they were all still possibles. The only person Dick didn't try to defend was Bill. And himself.

"How about me?" he asked.

"You?"

"Sure. Don't tell me you don't have stuff written down about me in that little notebook of yours?" He smiled and pushed back an unruly piece of brown hair from his eyes.

"Okay," I said, "I won't tell you."

He laughed but it wasn't mirthful.

"Did you do it?" I asked.

"Sure. I killed my best friend because underneath I really hated him."

"It seems everyone else did."

He waved a hand as if to brush away words. "They didn't know Kirk like I did."

I wondered if maybe he was the one who didn't know Kirk. "Dick, did Kirk tell you anything about me?"

"Of course. He told me everything. He was planning to tell Charlotte that night so he could be out in the open with you."

I felt a tug inside me. Even after everything I'd learned about Kirk, I obviously still cared. "Really?"

"Really. He told me right before the game."

"Funny he didn't tell me."

"He wanted to surprise you."

"I guess," I said. Why didn't I believe that? "You're sure?"

Dick laughed. "Sure I'm sure. He really loved you, Anna. Kirk was everything you thought he was."

I wanted that to be true, but how could I just discount what the others had told me? Confused, I turned to something new. "It must have been hard on you to be best friends with someone so perfect," I said.

He looked startled. "Not at all. Why do you say that?"

"Oh, I don't know."

"I guess if he'd been different—conceited or arrogant—it might have been, but Kirk was always great to me."

I remembered that first night and that Dick had gone along on Kirk's date with Charlotte. At the time I'd thought it very generous of him, but now, knowing he hadn't really cared for Charlotte, I didn't think it was so hot.

"Did Charlotte have a breakdown once, Dick?"

"Did Kirk tell you that?"

I nodded. "But Nicki, and Charlotte herself, said it wasn't true."

Again he dismissed my words with a gesture of his hand. "Nicki doesn't know anything and Charlotte's not about to admit it. Take my word for it, Anna, she had a breakdown. And it was bad. Kirk never loved her. He was just being nice to her."

"If he didn't love her, then why did he steal her away from Watson?"

He looked shocked. "He never did. He didn't have to. I mean Charlotte and Watson were chums, but nothing more. They grew up together, right next door. Of course maybe Watson had other ideas I wouldn't know anything about."

I didn't know what to believe. I went back to how he felt about Kirk. "Weren't you ever jealous of him?"

"Okay, you got me," he said. "I hate to admit it, especially now with him dead but, well, yes. Sure I was. I'd have to be weird not to be, I guess."

I felt a sense of relief. Dick had been sounding too good to be true.

"You would. My best friend where I used to live made me jealous sometimes. There's nothing wrong with that," I confided.

"It makes me feel lousy. I mean to be jealous of your best friend. But Kirk was always the smartest and the best-looking. He got the best marks without studying, and made the football team at college first year. Hardly anybody does that. And he always got the best girls . . . like you," he said, looking down into his coffee cup like something important was going on there.

I felt odd. I wanted to leave. Finishing my coffee, I said, "Well, it seems normal to me for you to have been jealous."

"I never told anyone that before."

"Thanks for trusting me," I said. "I think I'd better go now."

He looked at his big, square watch. "Yes, me too."

Since we would be seeing each other shortly at the restaurant, there were no big good-byes; we went our separate ways to our cars. I sat in mine and added some notes under Dick's name. I hadn't had a motive for him before, but now I did. Jealousy. It didn't seem terribly strong, and I wondered if he would've admitted it to me if he'd killed Kirk. I noticed too, that in my previous notes I'd remarked that Dick had seemed eager to pin the murder on Tony, but today he'd seemed content to let the guilt lie with Bill. I wondered why he'd given up so easily on Tony. Both Tony and Bill were outsiders, so maybe it didn't make any difference to him which one it was as long as the suspicion didn't fall on any of the natives. I was almost sure that was true.

I closed my notebook, put it away and started the car. Something was nagging at me, something I couldn't identify. It was like having a dream you couldn't quite remember but knew you should. Oh, well, I thought, maybe it would come back.

At the restaurant my mother greeted me with:

"Let's see your shells."

"I don't have any."

"What? All this time you've been shell hunting and you didn't find one? Tsk, tsk, what a shame." She crossed her arms over her chest, thrust out one hip and stared at me.

"Okay, okay," I said. "I didn't go shell hunting."

"NO! I don't believe it."

"Will you stop, Mom." I hated it when she played that game. "There was something I had to do, that's all."

"And you're not going to tell me about it, right?"

"Right."

"Okay. But from now on don't ask your brother to

lie for you—he's in enough trouble already." She walked away.

I knew she was ticked off, but there was not much I could do about it without telling her exactly what was going on. From now on I'd have to be careful, because Mom was no dope and I knew she'd be watching me, wanting to know what was happening. I went right to work on some steamers while I thought over all I'd learned.

Much later I got to talk to Larry. We took a break at the same time and went down to the beach. It wasn't a very starry night, but the moon was visible from time to time when it appeared from behind the clouds.

Knowing we didn't have a whole lot of time, I told him what I'd heard about his fight with Kirk and asked him right out what it was about. He didn't say anything for a while and then I heard him sniffling. I looked over and saw that he was crying. I felt like a rat.

"Gee, Larry, I didn't mean to make you cry."

"Doesn't matter," he said.

I reached in my front pocket and took out my notebook and a tissue, which I handed him.

"Thanks. Who told you about the fight?"

I opened the notebook. "Let's see," I said, flipping through pages pretending to look for the answer. I couldn't see anything, but Larry was too upset to realize that.

"It says here it was Watson who told me."

"What is that thing?"

191

"It's my murder notebook. I have stuff in here about everyone."

"Me?"

"Yes, you, too," I said, trying to sound a little ashamed of what I was doing.

"Can I see it?"

"Afraid not." I put it back in my pocket.

"Watson," he said strangely. "That's right. I remember now, when I ran out I saw him but it didn't, you know, sink in."

"What was the fight about?" I asked again.

"Just something Kirk wanted me to do that I didn't want to do."

"But what?"

"Why should I tell *you*, Anna?"

I hadn't counted on that response. Everybody else had been so cooperative. That thought gave me an idea. "Everyone else has answered my questions. When you're innocent I guess you're not afraid to talk."

"Listen, Anna, don't bug me, okay? What are you, anyway, some kind of private eye or something?"

I felt like a real jerk but I wanted to know the answer to my question. The only chance I had, I felt, was to turn the tables on him. I got mad and jumped up. "Okay, Larry, okay." I yelled. "If it was your brother who was arrested, you might think differently." I started to walk away.

"Wait a minute," he called.

I smiled to myself. I was getting good at this. Just like Libby Crawford. I stopped and waited for him to come over to me.

"I forgot about Bill, I'm sorry, Anna. I'll tell you if you think it'll help."

I realized then that he didn't understand that whatever he said might incriminate him, but I wasn't about to tell him. I just said, "It might help, you never know."

"Okay then. I know you liked my brother a lot, but you didn't really know him."

There it was again.

Larry went on. "Last summer I wanted a computer more than anything else in the world. Kirk knew that. Well, I guess you see by now that you don't make that much money here."

"I wondered how you'd saved so much."

"I didn't. I mean not from working here. I sold pot to my friends. Pot that Kirk gave me to sell."

"Kirk was a dealer?" I asked incredulously.

"Yes. Except he never really approached anyone. He made me do that."

"*Made* you?"

"Well, not last year. I wanted to do it then because I wanted that computer. I knew it was a rotten thing to be doing, and I didn't want any part of it *this* summer. But he threatened me, said he'd tell and it would really make my dad's last months a nightmare. So I gave in. Then that night, the night he was killed, he told me he wanted me to start selling cocaine. I wasn't going to do that. No way. Again he said he'd tell Dad and I just went crazy. My poor dad, you know. I jumped Kirk then, tried to beat him up, but it was stupid. He was much bigger and stronger than me and he just laughed. I ran out then. That's it. That's all there was."

193

My head was reeling. Could this really be true? Kirk selling pot, cocaine? "Are you telling me the truth, Larry?"

"I swear it. I swear it on my father's life."

I believed him. "You said you wished Kirk was dead."

"Yes, and I did wish it. But you say things, you know."

"Are you sorry he's dead?"

There was a long silence and I tried to see Larry's face, but it was too dark. Finally he spoke.

"I didn't kill him, Anna, but I don't miss him. I'm glad he won't be around to torture me anymore. I'm only sorry it had to happen now . . . so Dad had to know."

"Did anyone else know about the drugs? I mean, that Kirk was behind it?"

"No. I never told anybody."

So then, it could all have been a lie. "Well, thanks, Larry, thanks for telling me."

"You going to tell anyone?"

"Not unless I have to."

"Meaning?"

"If I find out you did it."

"I didn't."

"Then I won't tell."

We left the beach and went back to work. Larry certainly had a motive, but his opportunity was pretty slim. Still, it was possible.

The trouble was, everybody had a good motive and I felt no closer to an answer than I ever had. When work was over Bill and I would look for the gloves. If we found them we'd go to Smolley with them. But not until I set a trap. Tomorrow I would leave my notebook somewhere, like bait waiting for a lobster, and see who bit.

194

19

After work Bill and I told Mom and Dad that we were going into Cranberry Harbor to have some pizza. Mom gave me a kind of skeptical look but I told her I hadn't eaten any dinner, which was true, and finally she bought it. Dad was so upset about Bill, he just seemed out of it most of the time and went along with whatever Mom decided.

There was one tricky moment when Kate was angling to come along with us, but Mom put the kibosh on that. So Bill and I hopped into his car and drove off. Actually we were both starving, so we went to McDuff's Pizza Parlor (they did not make Irish pizza despite the name) and ordered a large pie with pepperoni and extra cheese.

While we ate we reviewed the case. I filled Bill in on the stuff I'd learned about Watson, Dick and Larry, and he told me that he'd been able to casually drop the information to Charlotte and Nicki that I had a notebook filled with stuff about everyone.

"So," I said, "it looks to me like there are five suspects." I had torn up my notes about Bill because I just knew he couldn't have done it. No matter how much he cared for Nicki, Bill could never kill anyone.

"Five?" he asked, a long string of cheese going from his mouth up to the wedge of pizza he held above his head.

"Five," I repeated. "I know you didn't do it."

"I wasn't thinking of me. How about Tony?"

"Oh." I had practically forgotten Tony existed. "Where do you suppose he is?"

"Got me." The cheesy string disappeared.

"I guess he's totally mad at me."

"Probably."

I felt bad about Tony, but I'd had no other choice and for all I knew he was the killer. But something about that idea didn't exactly sit well with me. It was hard to believe I'd been so fooled by *two* guys. But then, on the other hand, if one fooled me why not two?

"All right," I said, "six suspects."

"Who do you think had the most motive?" Bill asked.

"They all do," I answered, finding it very frustrating.

"Tomorrow should tell the tale when you leave your notebook around."

"I hope so. I don't think I can take the suspense much longer. You know, it's funny, sometimes I think I almost have the answer. It's there and then it's not. You know what I mean?"

"No."

196

"Great. Well, anyway, I feel like that. Libby Crawford goes through that all the time and then it just comes to her, you know? Everything falls into place at the right moment."

"Anna, Libby Crawford is not a real person," Bill said, looking at me like I was crazy.

"I know *that*. But even so she's a good guide."

"Yeah, and she almost gets killed in every book."

"Well, like you said, Bill, it's not real."

"Maybe we should just tell Smolley about the gloves. I mean, what's the point of us going into the woods looking for them anyway?"

"You know he won't listen."

"Yeah, I guess you're right."

"But if we can show him that somebody used gloves, then maybe he'll realize it wasn't you. I mean, if you'd done it using gloves then your prints wouldn't have been on the knife, right?"

"Right."

"Right. Eat up," I ordered.

We finished off the pizza and drove back to the restaurant. Inside the cabin we each got a flashlight and started toward the woods where we'd played the game. The night was dark—no stars—and a wicked wind from the east was kicking up.

Shivering, Bill said, "Maybe we shouldn't do this tonight."

"Now or never," I said.

"The weather's getting lousy," he protested.

"Let's hurry then."

"What if a fog comes in?"

"It won't."

"Looks like it might."

"Oh, come on, Bill, let's just get it over with."

"Okay," he said reluctantly.

We started toward the woods, flashlights in hand. When we got to the edge, I said, "I think we should separate. You go to the right and I'll go to the left. We'll make a circle and meet at the tree where . . . where it happened, okay?"

"Okay."

The moment Bill was out of sight I was sorry we'd arranged it that way. I don't mind saying I was suddenly scared to death. Every hoot of an owl, every creak of a branch made me jump, swinging my light around in wild arcs. And then I saw it creeping along the ground.

Fog.

Bill had been right.

Fog in Maine is like nowhere else, I think. It's iron gray and cold. And it looks like smoke. Steadily it moved in and upward. I saw it coming at me like something alive and deadly. In seconds it had gone from the height of my ankles to the tops of the trees. It was like a curtain of death, relentless and opaque. I felt it with a rush of sudden cold and wetness, and I wanted to scream but knew it was pointless. My flashlight couldn't even begin to penetrate it and, in fact, seemed to bounce off the hideous stuff as if it was solid. I panicked and was afraid to move in any direction. I had to call for my brother.

"Bill," I yelled, "Bill where are you?"

There was no reply. We were too far away from each other. And even if he heard me there would be nothing for him to do. He wouldn't be able to get to me through this fog any more than I could get to him.

My hands felt wet, my clothes soaked. The fog seemed to collect and condense on my face and it dripped down my neck. I took a step or two to my right and felt I was walking through water. There was no use. I'd have to stand still and wait for it to lift. That knowledge was chilling. This kind of fog could last for hours. I began to cry. Why had I insisted on doing this? Why hadn't I listened to Bill? I was always so bullheaded, intent on my own way. Well, now I'd really done it. I swore I'd never do something like this again. I would listen to reason and let others take the chances.

A rustling interrupted my thoughts. It had sounded like footsteps. I whirled around and pointed my flashlight in the direction from which I'd heard the noise. It was futile; I could see nothing but the fog itself. And then I heard a swishing sound from behind me. I twirled around.

"Bill?" I asked, my voice shaking. "Bill, is that you?"

Another sound, closer, louder. I was sure I felt the presence of another person.

"Bill?" I called again, whimpering now. "Answer me."

My answer came in the form of a crack on my skull. At first it bewildered me. As I dropped the flashlight, my knees buckled and I reached out, my hands sliding down something hard and slick. I couldn't imagine what was happening, and in the split second it took before it was over I felt like I was in a dream or falling through space somehow. Then just before everything went black, I registered that someone had hit me on the head . . . hard.

"Anna? Anna, darling?"

I opened my eyes. I was in my room, in bed, and Mom was calling me. I was confused, but then everything came back to me like a kaleidoscope making its pattern.

The fog had lifted and I had awakened to find Bill next to me, tears in his eyes. He'd looked at my head and found no blood, just a bump the size of an egg. We'd made our way back to his car. Halfway home I discovered that my notebook was missing from my front pocket. It was then we understood the reason for the attack.

At the house we tried very hard to come in quietly, but at the foot of the stairs I passed out again. And now here I was.

"Mom," I said.

She took my hand. "You dope. Since when are you a detective?"

"I don't know, Mom—I just thought I could help Bill."

"You've only succeeded in causing more trouble, more worry," Dad said.

"I'm sorry," I said.

"Sorry doesn't change anything," he answered.

"Come on, Jack," Mom said, "she's paying a high price as it is." She turned back to me, stroking my hand. "The doctor says you should stay in bed for at least a week. You probably have a concussion."

I remembered the doctor then. I'd awakened some time back and he'd been there with his little light shining in my eyes.

"What time is it?" I asked.

Mom looked at her watch. "Almost one," she said.

It was dark, so I knew it was still night. "I have to sleep," I said.

"Of course you do."

She leaned over me and I felt her warm lips on my cheek. It made me feel good, loved, secure. Then I heard my parents' footsteps cross the hard wood floor, the opening of the door, the closing. I fell asleep.

Waking with a start, I sat straight up in bed, my head hurting like crazy. Again all the events of the night slowly came back to me. I leaned into the pillows. Dawn was just breaking. I refocused on my dream. It was hazy the way dreams are, distorted and blurry. I was somewhere in a field and all the kids were there: Nicki, Watson, Larry, Dick, Charlotte, Bill and Tony. They were in a semicircle and I was at the center facing them. Suddenly Kirk appeared, floating through the air. I know who did it, I thought, opened my mouth to name the person, and that was when I had awakened.

I tried desperately to get back inside the dream but I couldn't. I was convinced that if I could remember what I'd thought just before I'd woken up, I'd have the answer. But it was no use—that part of the dream kept going to dust like a crushed moth.

I reviewed what I knew, making a mental list (not in order of suspicion) in my head.

1. NICKI—motive: anger because of what Kirk had made her do.
2. DICK—motive: jealousy and envy of everything Kirk had. Tired of being Kirk's yes man.
3. WATSON—motive: anger at Kirk stealing Charlotte (even if it wasn't true, he believed it). And don't forget the incredibly evil picture he drew of Kirk.
4. LARRY—motive: anger and rage over drug thing and blackmail.
5. CHARLOTTE—motive: anger at the way Kirk treated her and his relationship with me.
6. TONY—motive: jealousy of Kirk and me.

Once again I couldn't see where one person looked more guilty than the others. If only I knew who had stolen the notebook. And then I remembered something.

It was right after I'd been knocked on the head. I was falling and my hands reached out to find a hold. It was then that I touched something odd, yet something familiar. Hard. Slick. Something made of rubber. All at once I knew who had knocked me out, taken the notebook and killed Kirk. There was only one way to prove it. I had to find the notebook.

Slowly, I swung my legs over the side of the bed and stood up. I was not too steady. I waited a moment until my head cleared and I felt a bit better. My clothes were on a chair and, as if underwater, I dressed.

I walked to my bedroom door and gingerly opened it. There was no light coming from under any door. I crept down the stairs, remembering how I'd done this

202

with Tony days before. But this time I was even more scared.

The front door was locked, but I managed to get it open with a minimum of noise. My car was still back at the restaurant. I would have to use Bill's. Usually he left his keys in the car and I prayed he'd done so last night. He had. Now came the tricky part. Starting the car without waking anyone was going to be a miracle. I got in noiselessly, not shutting the door securely, turned the key partway, pressed down on the accelerator, held it and turned the key farther. The motor caught. I sucked in my breath.

I released the brake and very carefully depressed the gas pedal again after I put the car into drive. I moved forward, the early-morning sun making it light enough for me to see without putting on lights. At the top of the road I expelled my breath. I'd gotten away with it. My head hurt, but for the moment I didn't feel dizzy. I said a silent prayer that I'd make it there before my eyes went out of focus again. Briefly I remembered my earlier vow to not take chances anymore, and then I dismissed it, telling myself, next time . . . next time I wouldn't take chances. I had no idea what I meant by next time and didn't care.

Slamming shut my door, I turned onto Route 1. It was almost over.

20

When I got to Watson's road I cut the motor and coasted down the hill. Then I parked behind some trees and walked the rest of the way. A few yards from his truck I stopped, waiting and listening. The only sounds were those of early, early morning: birds and insects. It was just as I'd thought it would be. Watson was out hauling traps, and I had a clear field to search for the notebook.

Amazingly my head seemed clear, not a sign of dizziness, although I still had a pain where Watson had conked me. I had no doubts now that he was the one. When I had fallen and reached out for purchase, I'd grabbed a pair of legs. Legs that felt hard and slick because they were wearing . . . waders.

The first place I was going to look for the notebook was in his art folder, which he kept in his truck. I wished I had someone to bet with that it would be there, I was that sure. I opened the door on the driver's side and winced at the screaking sound it made. That really hurt my head! I climbed up on the running board and felt around under the seat until my hand touched cardboard. The folder was there. My heart began to beat faster. I pulled it out and laid it on the seat. Quickly I riffled the sheets of paper, trying not to be distracted by the beautiful artwork. How could someone so talented, so sensitive, be a killer? Well, it was nothing new. Convicts were always having art shows and writing books, weren't they?

I came to the terrible portrait of Kirk and I was shocked all over again. I turned it over, unable to look at it. Then I flipped through four more sheets and found myself at the end of the folder. I couldn't believe it. No notebook. Could I have missed it? Stupidly I sifted through all the pages again but found nothing. Okay. He must have hidden it in the shack. I put the folder back, closed the door of the truck and started down the path.

My confidence was shaken slightly. Still, I wasn't about to give up. The shack's door was closed but unlocked as usual. I pushed it open. The room was much darker than last time because of the hour. Stepping in I was again assaulted by the smell of old bait. It made me cough. I didn't shut the door completely because I needed the light and the air. There was no danger, I thought, of Watson returning so early, but other fishermen might notice if I left the door wide open.

Glancing around I could see most of the shack's corners and everything in it. Back against the far wall was the large metal box. I headed right for it.

I knelt down on the hard dirt floor and opened the box. There were three tiers of trays, and I figured the notebook would be at the bottom. I removed the first tray, which held hooks and stuff, and put it on the floor. The second tray had in it nylon line and some rope handles for lobster traps. I took that out, too. There was one more tray, the largest, and it held tools. It would be heavy, I knew. As I was reaching for it I heard a squeaking sound. I stopped moving and waited. The only sound I heard was my own breathing. My back was to the door, but when I turned my head I saw the shack as it had been when I entered. The wind, I decided, had blown the door on its rusty hinges. I went back to work and removed the bottom tray. My spirits sank to a new low. There was nothing on the bottom of the box. I began to replace the trays when I heard another sound . . . like a footstep. This time I held my breath, afraid to turn. But what I heard was more footsteps. And then they stopped. My mind reeled and my heart thundered against the wall of my chest. Someone was standing behind me!

If you've ever been on a roller coaster, then you know what happened to my stomach at that point. I didn't know what to do. Myriad excuses skidded through my mind to give to Watson for my being there, going through his fishing box. All of them seemed stupid. Meanwhile I'd have to think of something to stall him and try and get us both out of the shack.

Slowly, my blood making crashing noices in my ears, I rose. And then I turned.

"Dick!" I cried, surprised and relieved.

"Hello, Anna."

"Oh, Dick, I'm so glad you're here. I thought it was Watson and . . ." I stopped, my sense of relief swiftly reverting to panic. Three questions came into my mind like flashes on a neon sign:

1. What was Dick doing here?
2. Why was he wearing gloves?
3. Why was he wearing waders?

Even I, the world's *worst* detective, knew what these things meant. How could I have been so wrong? Never mind that, I told myself; think of how to get out of this one. I decided to go on pretending that I didn't know he was the killer.

"What are you doing here?" I asked innocently, while slowly moving toward the door.

Subtly he moved in front of me, blocking my way.

"I wanted to talk to you," he said.

"But how did you know where I was?" I inched to my left.

He inched right along with me.

"I've been following you," he said directly.

I continued to feign innocence. "Really? How come?" I tried a careful move to the right, but Dick stayed with me. My breathing quickened.

"I wanted to talk to you, Anna."

"What about?"

"About this." He pulled my notebook from inside his shirt.

"Oh, there it is," I said cheerfully. "I wondered where it had gotten to."

"Cut it out," he commanded in a dark voice.

I sucked in my breath as if he'd slapped me. I was convinced now that I wasn't going to get out of this alive. Why hadn't I kept my promise to myself? What a jerk I was. But I couldn't just let him . . . what? What would he do to me? Would he stab me as he had Kirk?

He waved my notebook in front of me. "Why did you have to do this?" he asked, his eyes looking oddly sad.

"Do what?" I stalled.

"Don't make me mad, Anna."

I felt his threat like hands around my throat, "Okay. I'm sorry."

"You have no understanding of my reasons. None."

I decided I might as well hear what he had to say even if I was going to die. "Tell me then," I suggested.

"You think I was jealous of Kirk because you're jealous of *your* friend."

"You told me you were, Dick."

"Because that's what you wanted to hear. I knew what you were doing, what you were after, why you were asking so many questions. Do you think I'm stupid?"

"Of course not," I said. Maybe flattery would help. "I've always thought you were very smart, smarter than anyone."

"Not smarter than Kirk. Nobody is. Was. But I had to do it, Anna. He'd changed."

"Changed?" He was very into himself now, and when I moved a little bit to the left he didn't move with me. I got the smallest ray of hope.

"Yes. Kirk was always special, always number one in everything, and . . ."

208

"And what were you?" I asked, moving again. He didn't notice.

"Me? I was number two but I didn't mind. That was just how it was and I accepted it. All our lives it had been that way, since we were children. Kirk was head honcho and I was his sidekick. Do you think that bothered me? It didn't. When my dad said, 'Why can't you be more like Kirk?' I just shrugged, because I knew Kirk was an original and nobody could be like him. I was just glad to be his friend."

"I can understand that," I lied.

"Can you?"

I nodded.

"No, I don't think you can. How could you? You're one of those special people: good-looking, smart, popular. Like Kirk. But I'm not like that. I never was. You think I never looked in a mirror or something?"

I didn't know what to say. Even under these circumstances I knew it would be pointless to try and tell him he was handsome, so I got him back on Kirk. "What did you mean, Kirk changed?"

"Well, it wasn't so much that he'd changed, I guess. More like he'd crossed some kind of invisible line. See, Kirk was always mischievous and . . ."

"Mischievous?" I had a feeling it was more than that.

Dick pushed a piece of hair from his eyes. "Just little things like breaking a window or initiating some kid into our club, and sometimes he'd get carried away, go too far. I never minded taking the blame because—"

"Wait a minute. You took the blame for things Kirk did?"

He looked surprised. "Of course. It was only fair."

"How'd you figure that?"

A look of fury crossed his face. "Aren't you listening? I told you. I was just a nobody until Kirk made me his friend. Besides, that was the agreement. I swore I would do whatever he asked. I signed my name in blood. It was fair, it really was. But then everthing started to get out of hand."

"You mean like him taking Charlotte away from Watson when he didn't even care about her?"

"Exactly."

"And taking those pictures of Nicki and selling them?"

"Yes, that's right. I tried not to notice, not to care, but I couldn't keep pretending he wasn't doing those things. You understand, don't you?"

"Of course I do, Dick," I lied. Maybe if I just went along with everything he said, there'd be a chance. Maybe I wouldn't have to make a try for the hammer that was hanging on the wall just within my reach.

Suddenly his face contorted, the big nose giving him a hawklike appearance. "But you want your brother cleared, don't you?"

I couldn't lie about that but I didn't have to answer either. Then I put a couple of two and twos together. "You were the one who told Smolley that Bill'd been in trouble before, weren't you?"

"It was my duty, Anna. Someone had to do it."

"Yeah, sure." I calculated that I could grab the hammer in an instant if I had to, as long as he let me stay where I was. I had to keep him talking, because if he talked long enough maybe someone would come. Maybe

210

Watson would come back, although it seemed too soon for that. Still, stalling for time was my only chance.

"So what happened, Dick?"

"When I heard Kirk laughing at Bill about the initials in the tree, it came to me. I knew Kirk had lent his knife to Bill and that his fingerprints would be on it."

"But how did you know you'd be able to get the knife so easily from Kirk?"

"He told me he was going to carve your initials and his in a tree during the game and then tell Charlotte to go look at it."

I felt a wave of humiliation.

"I knew I had to do it that night or never. Everything was perfect. I might not get another chance like that. Do you understand?"

"Yes, I do," I said softly, trying to make him think I was on his side. And then I realized something. The thing that had been nagging me, the thing I hadn't been able to put into place, now rang in my ears loud and clear.

When I had been questioning Dick the day before, he'd said something that bothered me but I hadn't known what it was. Now I knew. If only I'd placed it then, I wouldn't be in this jam.

"You followed Kirk the night of the murder, didn't you? And you were watching him, watching us. I saw you earlier moving around after the whistle, but I thought you'd just gone from one tree to another."

"It was *you* I was following. Kirk had told me you were going to meet."

"That's why you said Larry would have had to wait

211

nearby for *two* minutes before I left. Only the killer would have known how long I'd stayed with Kirk before I started for home base. You gave yourself away then, Dick."

He smiled crookedly. "But you didn't pick up on it, did you?"

"I almost did," I said feebly.

"But you didn't," he insisted. "And now it's too late."

My heart plummeted. "What do you mean?"

"You don't think I'm going to let you tell everybody I'm the killer, do you?"

Quickly, stalling for time again, I said, "Those gloves you're wearing . . . are they Larry's?"

"Of course. I needed gloves so my prints wouldn't be on the knife, and naturally I couldn't use my own. I just grabbed a pair."

"And the waders?"

"Everyone who's grown up on Blue Haven owns a pair of waders, Anna."

"But you wanted me to think you were Watson, didn't you?"

"Exactly. You're so smart it's a shame you have to die."

"I promise I won't say anything. Honest Injun," I said, reverting to childhood as Dick moved closer to me.

"No, Anna. I can't take that chance."

He lunged then, the gloved hands coming toward my throat, bigger and bigger. I didn't try to run or dodge him because I knew it wouldn't work. I stayed in place, shaking to pieces but it was my only chance. At the moment his hands touched my throat and he was look-

212

ing into my eyes, I reached for the hammer, got it, and slammed him on the side of the head. He went down like a sack of flour.

Quickly I jumped over him and found myself flying through the air and into the arms of Tony! Behind him was the figure of Harvard Smolley. Stunned, I began to cry and then everything blurred as I passed out.

21

Well, I've been in bed for a week now and Tony has visited every day. Mom and Dad think he's the neatest thing since sliced bread. You see what a little saving of the maiden can do?

Actually, he didn't really save me. I saved myself. But if Mom and Dad want to think of Tony as a hero, who am I to tell them they're wrong? On the other hand, I was awfully glad he was there.

It seems that when Bill and I went into the woods to look for the gloves, Tony was following us and, of course, so was Dick. We must have all looked pretty silly creeping around in that fog! Anyway, Tony lost me so he didn't even know about Dick bopping me on the head. But after Bill and I had left the area, and the fog lifted, he saw Dick go to a culvert and remove a pair of gloves. Well, Tony had no idea what that was about, but it seemed suspicious to him. So, thinking that Smolley was after *him*, he went to him with the information.

Smolley knew what had happened to me and he'd also paid attention to what I'd said about the person who'd told about Bill stealing also being the killer. So with Tony he put two and two together. But they didn't really have proof. Smolley told Tony to go home and sleep and they'd talk later. But no way was Tony about to sleep. He was too worried about me.

I feel pretty guilty about having thought Tony was the murderer. I must have been crazy. Still, I told him I didn't want him saying any more stuff to me like he did the night of the prom. He said he'd always been sorry about that and he'd never do a dumb thing like it again.

Even though Tony knows about me and Kirk, he still wants me back. I think that's pretty neat of him, but I've decided to be single for a while. Mom says I've been through a lot, more than some people go through in a lifetime. The thing is, I need some time to think over everything that's happened, to kind of sort out my feelings and just be with myself. There'll be plenty of time later for me and Tony if that's how it's supposed to be.

Anyway, after Tony left Smolley, he drove over to our house, hid his car and watched in case Dick showed up. And that was when he saw me take off for Watson's. So very carefully he followed me. Meanwhile Smolley was following Dick. Both Tony and Smolley heard the whole dialogue between Dick and me and ran in just as I was cracking Dick over the head with the hammer.

Dick's in the hospital with a concussion, and when

he's better I guess he'll be arraigned for murdering Kirk. Mom says being second best to someone he knew was rotten at the heart pushed him over the sanity line. I can't help feeling sorry for Dick. I keep thinking that if he'd been born somewhere else and never met Kirk, he might have been an okay guy. But Mom says something was off in him to start with, because another person would have just dumped Kirk a long time ago. I guess she's right, but that doesn't stop me from having sympathy for him.

Nicki came to see me yesterday and said she hoped we could be friends. I was very glad of that. And even Charlotte sent me flowers. She and Watson have gotten back together, according to Nicki. I'm really happy for them.

Also, Smolley is not going to arrest Larry for dealing. Tony said Smolley thinks, under the circumstances, it would do more harm than good. I think I underestimated Smolley, too. He's turned out to be pretty smart, after all.

My brother Bill, my twin, my friend, seems to be his old self again. I guess having Nicki as a girlfriend helps. And he doesn't seem to mind at all that she's two inches taller than he. He says all that means is there's just more of her to love! Me? I'll be getting out of this bed tomorrow, but not out of the house. Dad has grounded me.

He said, "I don't care if you solved the Jack the Ripper case, you still disobeyed us. So you're grounded for two weeks starting when you're better."

Mom wasn't as mad at me as she was curious. But she

almost flipped when I told her that I'd used Libby Crawford as my model.

"But, Anna," Mom said, "Libby always gets it wrong. I mean she only solves it by accident."

"Well," I said, "I wasn't trying to imitate her totally."

I've decided there's absolutely no reason anyone has to know that what I did was a *perfect* Libby imitation. I mean, what people don't know doesn't hurt them. Right?

Right.